Seasons of Change

'APR   2010

Seasons of Change

Rená A. Finney

www.urbanbooks.net

Urban Books, LLC
78 East Industry Court
Deer Park, NY 11729

ISBN 13: 978-1-60162-213-6
ISBN 10: 1-60162-213-9

First Printing May 2010
Printed in the United States of America

10 9 8 7 6 5 4 3 2 1

This is a work of fiction. Any references or similarities to actual events, real people, living, or dead, or to real locales are intended to give the novel a sense of reality. Any similarity in other names, characters, places, and incidents is entirely coincidental.

Distributed by Kensington Publishing Corp.
Submit Wholesale Orders to:
Kensington Publishing Corp.
C/O Penguin Group (USA) Inc.
Attention: Order Processing
405 Murray Hill Parkway
East Rutherford, NJ 07073-2316
Phone: 1-800-526-0275
Fax: 1-800-227-9604

"To every thing there is a season, a time for every purpose under heaven."

—Ecclesiastes 3:1

WINTER

"Winter dies into the spring, to be born again in the autumn."

—Marche Blumenberg

Prologue

Gabrielle

Once upon a time I thought I had the ideal family. I didn't consider myself to know a whole lot at my young age. After all, I was only eight years old. What I did know was, a lot of kids in my school, neighborhood, and church did not live in a two-parent home. I'd watch them at PTA meetings and other gatherings, and it always seemed like a part of them was missing.

Now, there was one girl who lived at the corner, right next door to Ms. Tilda, our church mother. Well, not really our mother, but she was the oldest woman in the church, and everyone who attended regularly called her Mother Tilda. Anyway, this girl told everyone she had two parents, except, I never saw her daddy. I always saw two women take her all over the place, and whenever I was close enough to hear her refer to them, I would hear her call both of them Mommy. All I could say was, she was one lucky girl. I didn't know another soul in the neighborhood or anywhere else that had two mothers. I was happy to have both my parents living under one roof, and many people told me I was blessed. And I believed them.

My mother, Deborah Price-Taylor, was, to me, the most beautiful woman in the world. She was the color of the pecans that fell off the trees in the backyard of our house, the prettiest color in the world. Mommy's hair fell over her shoulders in deep waves, and she was real tall, almost as tall as my Daddy. And, Daddy, well, many of my mom's family members called him Slick Taylor instead of Ed. I used to think it was because of his slick black hair that he always wore combed back and parted on the left side. Then I thought it could have been because he dressed real fine, like the men in the magazines I looked at when I went to the barbershop with him. Daddy was always as sharp as a tack in his alligator shoes and sharp hats that matched his outfits. He was a real dark brown man with skin that felt as smooth as silk. My face and body color fell somewhere between their two colors and made me feel like the best blend of Deborah and Ed.

I didn't fully understand what my cousins were saying when they called my daddy a first-class womanizer, but when one of them added one day that he chased after anything that had a skirt on, I decided that what they were saying wasn't good. They had some kind of nerve. They didn't know my Daddy and should have kept their noses out of our business. He was, to me, at that time, the best. Besides, he reminded us often, me and Mommy, that he worked hard on that big rig truck day and night to take good care of us and give us all the things we needed and almost all of the things we wanted. Dad would say, "Baby, your Mom folk just jealous 'cause I give y'all all these nice things," so I learned not to care about what they said.

Church for me was mandatory, not that I objected; it was the opposite really. I loved church, and interacting with all the members, both young and old. Everyone said I always had a way with people and was quite the social butterfly. I wasn't sure about the butterfly part, but I did like talking about anything to anybody at anytime, plain and simple. I'd been in church all my life, or at least as long as I could remember. Mom was on everything, constantly accepting any church-related invitation that came her way.

My dad used to come to church with us occasionally, but unfortunately as my mother's duties in the church increased, his limited attendance dwindled, and the one-sided arguments between them took place daily.

Mom never argued and took her vows and spiritual position as a submissive wife very seriously, doing everything for him despite the name-calling. When there was no response from the daily one-sided shouting episodes, Dad started using his oversized hands to get his point across.

I knew it was awful, my mother's tears and soft cries told me that her pain ran deep. But when it came to Ed and Deborah Taylor, I was too young to have a voice in grown folk business, so I didn't dare say a word or utter one sound. As much as I wanted to, there was no way I could speak against what I knew was hurting her. That's when the scale for me tilted from loving him completely to fearing that one day his anger would release its raging fury on me. Thankfully, it never did. I was never sure if it was because I was truly the apple of my daddy's eye, or if Cassie's constant presence in our home changed him.

Cassandra Price wasn't just my first cousin, she was my best friend. She had moved in with us right after my Aunt Cindy went on to a better place. All because of death. That was always such a scary, terrifying word and one I never thought I would have to deal with in my young age, at least not up close and personal. But the word intruded upon us and upset everything we knew as normal. It stormed in on a whirlwind of anguish, misery, pain, and devastation, and made its unwelcome presence known within my family circle. It took my Aunt Cindy away with a horrible disease called cancer, which was just too big for her to fight. It left behind the closest person to me, with no one to call mom, and no one to turn the world right side up whenever things turned upside down. That's where my mom, Deborah Price-Taylor, came in.

She became the substitute, even though we all knew that, for Cassie, no one could totally fill the void. Now, there was no end to our time together. She was now a part of the Taylor family.

Up until a few months before, the extra bed in my room was empty and only slept in when my parents allowed me to have a sleepover. Then, the comforter and canopy cover matched the one on my bed perfectly. But Cassie didn't like the color pink all that much, so Mom changed it to purple and I didn't mind at all. Everyone in the family always said we were as alike as two peas in a pod. I never understood what they meant, but they would laugh when they said it, so I knew it had to mean something good.

We arrived at church dressed in our puffy dresses, customary fold-down lace socks, and black, shiny, patent leather dress shoes. As was the usual routine, we went to the rear of the church and into the room elementary-age kids used for Sunday school.

"You want a Now and Later?" Cassie leaned over and handed me a grape Now and Later. She knew it was my favorite kind. It was hers too, but she only had one grape and one watermelon and offered me the better of the two.

I took the candy and smiled at her as the taste of grape filled my mouth. "We better eat these quick. You know we not suppose to have candy in church."

She nodded her head, affirming that she knew, but rolled her eyes, letting me know that she didn't really care. That was Cassie. While I was scared to do anything aside from what I was told I could do, she was the daring one and did the opposite of many of the things she was told.

"I know. You don't have to remind me of that every Sunday."

It was my turn to roll my eyes. I wanted to tell her she was right, and that every Sunday she still brought candy, when she wasn't supposed to.

We listened to the Sunday school lesson after all the kids were seated and quiet. I watched everyone in their own worlds, whispering and drawing on pieces of paper. The time went by slowly, because no one really wanted to answer any questions. Of course, both Cassie and I had spent many hours with my Bible scholar, Mom, and we knew almost every Bible character and could recite as many Bible verses as the grown folk at church. Heck, we lived church even when we weren't in church. But we remained as quiet as the others.

"Little Sister Gabby would you like to end our Sunday school with a prayer?" Sister Jones walked over and reached her hand toward me.

Everyone at the church called me Gabby, which my mom dubbed me, when she realized I was a little chatterbox. I remember my mother telling me that my grandmother said it was because I had an old soul. I didn't ask what that meant. Just assumed it was a good thing to have.

I stood beside Cassie, who was grinning from ear to ear, obviously glad that I was the one put on the spot and not her. There was a Bible verse that referred to being ready, and today, like so many other days, she wasn't. Whenever she was singled out, Cassie would bashfully decline and promise to do it next time. Cassandra "Cassie" Price could be a true dramatic piece of work when she wanted to be. I'd double dare anyone else to say that about her, but I could because I'd earned the right as her best friend.

"Yes, I sure can." I playfully rolled my eyes at Cassie before Sister Jones turned back toward me.

On top of knowing as many Bible verses as any grown person in church, I could pray just as well. Mom had taught me well. I wasn't always eager, but she'd taught me and Cassie to always have a willing spirit. At least one of us remembered that lesson, 'cause, when it came to Cassie, the lessons had sure enough fell on deaf ears.

After I carried out Sister Jones' request to pray, I helped out with the collection and handed it over to the ladies who handled the Sunday school finance business. When I had finished those tasks, I joined the other Little Saints choir members, who were seated in the front two pews of the choir loft, directly in front of the minister of music. We would be singing a couple of selections at the request of the pastor.

I sat back against the hard surface of the pew seat and took in my surroundings. The sanctuary was large and newly remodeled, with enough seats for all the people that came to enjoy the weekly services. It was so many more people than when I was younger. It seemed people liked the preaching, the singing, but not many of them liked offering time. They must not have heard the pastor tell us offering time was happy time. I watched some of them slip out past the ushers, toward the bathroom, their index finger up, but I never saw them come back in.

I waved back at some of the members who waved and smiled at me. My face was always plastered with a smile, and even when I didn't feel like it, I put on a happy face. It came from years of practice and watching my Mom interact and exchange pleasantries, regardless of how she felt, or the mood she was in. It was as if she got up in the morning with her mind made up to be jovial, and she expected me to do the same, regardless of what I felt deep down.

Sunday school ended, and I watched as bodies began running back and forth to make sure everything was ready for praise and worship to officially begin. The organist keyed up the music to let the team know it was time to get in position.

After a few minutes, the usher stationed at the side door

to the pulpit opened it wide, and everyone stood up as the deacons, ministers, and the armor bearer walked out slowly, making way for the pastor of Mt. Calvary Baptist Church. Adorned in a purple pastoral robe accented in gold braided trim, the pastor took the rightful place behind the large cherry oak podium and began singing along with the praise and worship team.

The new girl, Robin, looked up at my mom, who entered the sanctuary wide-eyed from admiration, and then she leaned over with a toothless grin on her face and whispered, "Don't you want to be just like your mom when you grow up?"

I looked directly at the girl, who was a few years younger than me, and before I could answer, my mind stilled. I considered her question, and thought about my life.

I blinked and reached to rub my eyes. My body shivered, it was so chilly in the room. I couldn't believe how cold I was.

I glanced over, expecting to see Cassie spread out in the bed. Instead, the comforter was at the end of the bed, and her robe was missing. I thought maybe she would have been snuggled between Mom and Dad, leaving me all alone down the hall to fight off the bogeyman, but when I tiptoed to their room and slowly opened the door, all I saw was my mother sleeping on her back, snoring softly.

As I made my way to the stairs, I started to get scared, thinking that someone in the family had taken Cassie to live with them. The thought made me speed up. I started down the steps and stopped midway when I saw Daddy in his recliner near the fireplace. His chair was facing the staircase, but his attention wasn't focused on who could be coming down the stairs.

I moved back a little to make sure he didn't realize I was out of bed when I should have been fast asleep, and saw Cassie sitting on his knee with her head down. Maybe she had been crying and my dad was telling her that everything would be all right. That had to be why he was rubbing her back with one of his big, wide hands, while the other hand was wrapped around her body.

Instead of going to them, I leaned forward slightly so I could hear what they were saying. My heart skipped a beat when I thought of the worst. Maybe he was telling her that she couldn't live with us anymore, or something more horrible that I couldn't even imagine. I couldn't stand the thought of Cassie being sent to live with someone else when she needed me to take care of her. I pressed my head against the opening in the rails, not wanting to miss a word.

"Cassie, you've got to keep our secret. You are special to me, and I love you so much." Dad placed her head on his big shoulder. "No one would understand, so you can't tell a soul." He kissed her cheek.

Cassie wrapped her arms around his neck, but it didn't look like the first time. It seemed they were familiar with the touches and feels that should have been awkward.

They had not displayed this kind of show for anyone's eyes, yet here they were, cuddled up, and Cassie's head was where my head was so often. I didn't want her head to be there. I didn't want her in his arms at all, because not only was I sharing, my Mom was sharing.

But there was something else. I didn't want them to have a secret, because secrets weren't good. And from what I could see, the secret between my best friend and Daddy wasn't good. Why else would it be talked about in the dark?

I couldn't move. I covered my mouth, wanting to make sure no noise would come out. Why was *my* Daddy holding Cassie like that? And why was he telling her he loved her, when he never ever told my Mom that? I needed to know, but yet I didn't want to know.

I knew my dad thought the world of me and called me his sweetie pie, but he had never uttered the words *I love you* to me.

That night their secret became my secret. As a result, I wrestled with what had been revealed in plain sight, and what held me captive in those moments of time, and what truth existed that I didn't know, and could never, ever accept.

Snapping out of the memory, I gathered a visual picture of my mom and coupled it all with the personal facts that had become our family history and the threads that held the Taylor family together. She was a beautiful lady, and everyone was so drawn to her. She in turn treated everyone with so much compassion and showered them all with love. It was so easy to love her. Everyone did, or at least, that is what I thought.

I breathed deeply and then exhaled. I spoke loud enough for Robin to hear me and soft enough not to bring attention to myself and have one of the ushers chastise me for speaking, or have my Mom see my lips move and give me the no-talking-in-church speech later.

"A little. But mostly I want to get married, have kids, and be happy all the time." I started to look away and added, "With no secrets."

Robin looked a little confused, but there was no time for another question. Pastor Deborah Price-Taylor was asking the congregation to stand.

Chapter 1

Cassandra

Nine Years Later

I was only eight years old when my mother died, and I went to live with my Aunt Debbie, Uncle Ed, and my cousin and best friend Gabby. We were inseparable, two peas in a pod, closer than close, and a lot closer than most. Gabrielle was my "shero," always thinking and believing that she was charged with coming in to save my day or help me make sense of the drama I often encountered. Some of it was my doing, and other times I carelessly walked right in with my eyes wide open. It was like seeing the bright, blinding light, hearing the high-pitched music that played right before the white girl in the scary movie got whacked and hearing a voice saying, "Don't walk in! Stay away!" And what did I do? I blinked my way through the light, turned a deaf ear to the *Freddy vs Jason* tune, ignored the voice and words of caution, and walked full speed ahead right into some mess. And yet Gabby was always there, from our adolescent days up until now. Most of the time she succeeded in getting me out of various situations and ordeals, and other times . . . well, let's just say, I was a true piece of work.

In the first few years after my mom died, I wondered if she would have been able to save me, if she would have been able to make my day or pick all the pieces up and put them back together again and in the right places. I wondered if my mom, Cindy had been equipped with some type of genetic "mother glue" that could seal my inner emotions and keep me from coming completely undone. Who knew?

Aunt Debbie tried her best to be the mother figure I needed, and God knows, she gave me all the love that an aunt could give. Many days she was able to help me make sense of an otherwise crazy world. I challenged her often, and still she was able to pick up the pieces and put them back together. They weren't always in the right place, but they weren't outside my being either.

But some things were impossible to fix or even forget. There was a gigantic, massive issue that I tried with everything in me to push back to the recesses of my mind. I'd even erected a brick wall around it, putting so many other things in front of it, and yet somehow it was always there. The good, the bad, and the ugly—That's what I called it. No amount of attention and affection afforded by my aunt, Gabby, and the rest of my family would ever give me what I needed the most, or make up for the state I was in.

Uncle Ed was always there and always doing, saying, and expressing, and I couldn't tell a soul, not even Gabby. All those years after my mom left me, he'd never stopped being what he obviously thought I needed. I never understood why he couldn't just be my Uncle Ed. Why couldn't he just play the uncle role and leave it at that? At seventeen years old, I still didn't understand. All I knew was that he was there, and every time he reminded me of it, a little more of me died.

Even in Cindy's death, I blamed her. Yeah, I had stopped calling her mom a long time ago, but Aunt Debbie wouldn't hear of it and corrected me every time. She finally left it alone and labeled it as part of my rebellious stage.

The stage that included the two-month period of smoking Virginia Slims that ended because I didn't like the taste, even though I thought it made me look ultracool. Then there was the crush I had on Kenneth and the days I skipped school to hang out with him. It ended because he couldn't French-kiss. I couldn't figure out how someone who talked the talk couldn't walk the walk. With him I was in no danger of losing my virginity, since he couldn't even get me warmed up or beyond first base.

There was the shoplifting I did once, all because Aunt Debbie didn't want to buy me and Gabby the latest jeans that everyone was wearing. I took matters into my own hands and hitched a ride to the mall. I waltzed in the store, smiling at the hired help there, asking questions about this shirt, belt, or whatever else caught my eye that day. Once they relaxed, thinking I was there only to shop, I checked the sizes and picked up two pairs of jeans, rolled them up, put them in my bag, and jetted. There was no way I was going to be sporting the latest and not have Gabby sporting right along with me.

It wasn't until two weeks later when I was called in by the gospel police, Pastor Deborah Price-Taylor, that I knew I was caught. She called me into her study and began talking about rights, wrongs, being proud of self, and pleasing Our Heavenly Father. I listened and threw my hands up, as if testifying and giving her the "go on, preacher woman" sway. Then the shoe fell. She told me that Sister James' big-mouth niece, Sharon, saw me steal some jeans from the mall. I thought she would make me do something humiliating, like take them back and apologize, or get up in church and tell the entire congregation, but she went down to the store and explained it all to the manager and paid for the two pairs of jeans.

For days I thought it was all a done deal, that the lecture was all the ordeal would cost me, until she drove me down to the children's home and informed me that I would be working there for free. For two months I slaved after school and every Saturday morning doing other people's dirty laundry. I washed, dried, and folded so many pieces of clothing, I felt like I was the number one employee at a labor camp. My only reprieve was watching Gabby sport her jeans and getting the compliments that both of us should have been receiving.

Aunt Debbie believed it all came from the hurt I felt deep down at losing my mother when I was so young and not old enough to understand death, dying, demise, decease, passing, expiration, curtains down, and lights out. Whatever they called it, Cindy was gone and would never return. News flash—That I understood. I couldn't say that was why I did what I did or acted like I acted, nor could I really say it wasn't. I just didn't know.

In between these events and skipping school just for the heck of it, I was a model student, and a positive teenager in the neighborhood and church. In fact, just a well-rounded young lady destined for great things. But it was the times I slipped that were the problem.

If I had a dollar for every time Aunt Debbie took me down to the church, closed the door to her office, and talked to me not as my aunt but as my pastor, I'd be rich. She'd even taken me to a child psychologist and spent good money to fix me, only to discover that what was wrong with me could never be fixed. It wasn't exactly broken, it just ceased to function.

After looking at inkblots, closing my eyes and pretending I was floating along in a big boat on the ocean with the birds singing and the wind blowing through my hair, I pretended the sessions were working for me. I reached down deep and pulled out my inner being and told myself I was okay with who I was. Time was the verbal prescription given to me by the psychologist as she diagnosed me.

I had become bitter toward Aunt Debbie. Even though she wasn't directly related to my problems, she was a player in the game. She just didn't know it. Gabby was my only outlet, and by the time I realized that overeating didn't pacify my hunger for acceptance, or whatever it was I was in search of and couldn't really identify, I was tipping the scales on the heavy side. Just what I needed, yet another problem.

By this time I needed someone else to reach a part of me that Gabby couldn't, and what wasn't being pacified through food. I needed to find refuge someplace safe. That's when Marco Phillip Brent came into the picture. He was as fine as his name sounded. Tall, dark, and handsome described my man to a tee. He had the prettiest sexy eyes and a bright smile. But, according to my Aunt Debbie and Uncle Ed, there was just one problem—he was a good-for-nothing. That's the way they put it. No, he wasn't born with a silver spoon in his mouth, and he wasn't one for the whole academic thing. However, he was at the top of the class in the school of hard knocks.

Marco told me often that he didn't choose his lifestyle, that the lifestyle chose him. I knew everyone thought he was a bad boy, because his reputation in our small town wasn't a good one, but it was all because of the company he kept. He just didn't want to turn his back on his friends and not be there to steer them in the right direction. I admired that about him. He was like the one that kept everybody out of trouble, and kept them from ending up in jail or on the streets with nothing.

I was the only one that he shared his story with, the only one that saw beyond the tough exterior, and allowed to get beyond the force field he put up around his life and his heart, for that matter. As much as people thought they knew Marco, they knew so very little. He kept it that way to protect himself from those that stood in judgment or felt he wasn't worth the time of day.

Marco was my song and I was his instrument. I loved him, and I believed he loved me. He had no family for me to impress, and while he wanted acceptance from mine, it didn't come. But I didn't care. What I did care about was being with him.

Just before my graduation, Marco said those three magical words that every girl yearns to hear. His reasoning had nothing at all to do with him feeling sorry for me or sentimental because of what I endured as a child. Nor did he try to convince me to be okay with something that I knew deep down was wrong.

Marco's saying "I love you" hadn't come as a verbal reward for sliding into home base. He had been patient with me and hadn't hounded me for sex like every other sex-crazed young boy who thought having sex would suddenly make them a man. There were plenty of them at school, and by the time no came out of my mouth, the attraction ended, and they were long gone.

It was never that way with Marco. A few times there had been heavy petting, hands in places where they shouldn't have been, and our tongues so deep in each other's mouth, we could feel each other's tonsils. The thing was, as much as I felt ready for the next logical step in our relationship, and I could see by the big bulge in his pants that he was too, he wouldn't let us go any farther. Maybe it was because he was nineteen years old. I wasn't sure. But it never seemed to bother him. He would just smile and tell me I was worth the wait.

How could I ever forget the Sunday morning Marco confessed his love for me? I was feeling a little under the weather and was home all alone when I decided to call him. The minute I heard his voice through the phone, the pain in my stomach went away, and I was just as eager to see him as he said he was to see me. What turned out as just a casual ride on his new bike ended up being the day I fell head over heels for him. It was the day he literally put me in orbit. My being anywhere close to a motorcycle was definitely not supposed to happen, but this was Marco, and I trusted him with my life. The thought of Aunt Debbie banning me from leaving the house crossed my mind for a quick second, and just as quickly as it crossed my mind, I dismissed it. Besides, I would have to get caught, and I didn't plan on getting caught.

We drove down by the water and just talked. We watched the boats leave and return to the dock and the waterfowl swim and come up to the water's edge, as if looking for something or making sure they could be seen. He held me tight, and I felt like nothing or no one could get to me.

"Baby, I've been going through some mess with my boys. The cops have been up in my spot two times this week already." He looked down on the ground.

I watched his jaw tighten and then relax a little. "What? Why the cops come to you?"

"Word on the street is that Toby and Sean been dealing for Rufus, and because they are my friends, everyone is assuming that they are hanging at my place or that I'm involved. I told my boys to get away from me with that mess. Then I hear they're telling people that their connection to Rufus is through me, that I'm running drugs for Rufus."

"Oh, Marco. How could they?" I reached out and rubbed his face just as he was turning away. I could tell how upset and disappointed he was. His friends were like his only family and meant a lot to him. How could any of them turn on him that way?

"I know. They are like my blood." Marco punched his fist into the open palm of his other hand.

My heart was breaking for him. In the past two years that I had been seeing him, he was as strong as a rock. I hadn't spent as much time with him as I would have liked, but whenever I could skip school, sneak away, or have Gabby cover for me, I was with him. Gabby didn't like it or him, but she never said a word to Aunt Debbie or Uncle Ed.

"What are you going to do?"

"I was thinking we could go away." He looked at me and searched my face for some kind of response.

"Go away? Marco, what in the world are you saying?" I backed up a few steps. I wasn't expecting him to say anything close to what I had just heard come out of his mouth. He knew I was planning to go to college to be a nurse. In fact, I had already been accepted on scholarship at a college across the bay, and we had talked about him visiting me there every weekend, and us finally being able to hang out as a couple.

"I'm sorry. I shouldn't have thought. I mean, I know you don't love me enough to go away with me."

It was his turn to back away. He turned his back to me and stared out over the water.

"I didn't say that. You know I love you." I walked toward him and gently touched his shoulder.

He turned slightly, and I saw tears.

"I shouldn't have asked you. What was I thinking, asking you to leave your family behind and be with me? In a few months you'll be going off to college with guys from all over, and you'll forget all about me."

"That's not true. I'm not going to college to be with anyone else. I want to be with you, but I just always thought we'd get married first."

I held my breath. I wasn't sure that marriage was what he had in mind once we went off into the sunset. I knew I probably sounded old-fashioned, or he likely thought I watched too much television. Wanting us to be one of those couples that they threw rice at and who'd drive off in a car decorated with a just married sticker on the bumper probably sounded like a fantasy or something straight out of a fairytale.

When I did decide to get married, I wanted the post-wedding, happily-ever-after plan. I wasn't sure it was what he wanted. Just this morning the only thing I was trying to figure out was which pumps to wear for the graduation ceremony. With all the uncertainty, there was one thing that I did know—I didn't want to be someplace that Marco wasn't.

"Of course, I want to get married. I would marry you today if the almighty Pastor Taylor would give us her blessing, but be real, Cassandra, she would never allow it to happen, not to mention your protective uncle. He turns up everywhere I am, all over town. Never says a word. Just watches me."

"They care about me, Marco. I've been through so much, and they have just always protected me. Aunt Debbie took me in, and I can't just forget that."

"I've heard all that before, but it's my turn now. I want to be the one protecting you. I'd love to buy you nice things and take you to the finest restaurants. We can't exactly have an open relationship, and I'm not complaining, but there is only so much you can do in two hours. Cassandra, I'm a grown man, and I need a grown woman."

"I know." I rubbed my neck, just thinking about the noose around it. Marco did always tell me that he wanted to do nice things for me, that he would love to take me to some beautiful, exotic places so far away from this humdrum, out-of-the-way town. I just wished they understood that he would never do anything to hurt me.

"Baby girl, I'm going to have to leave the area for a while. I'm not trying to get caught up in this mess. Once you're all settled in school, I'll visit you sometime."

Marco walked over to where his black-and-yellow Suzuki 750 was parked. He placed his black-and-yellow helmet on his head and reached for mine on the back of the bike. He'd had it airbrushed especially for me, and *Baby Girl*, his special nickname for me, was painted in black script and accented with yellow hearts.

Marco couldn't leave me. I didn't want to be without him. I didn't say a word as I put on my helmet, fastened it, got on the bike behind him, and held on tight as we took off. I leaned into his hard body and closed my eyes. The speed caused a steady breeze to touch my face, and as quickly as the tears fell, they were gone, leaving a chilly trace behind them.

We rode back home in complete silence, our individual thoughts humming along with the engine of the motorcycle, I guess. We passed houses so quickly, the trees and everything along the road became nearly invisible to me.

There was a pain and dull ache inside of me. It felt so much like when Cindy left me. Marco hadn't left, yet I was consumed with what his leaving me would feel like. This was my man, and he was going to leave and go God knows where. What if he met someone else and she was there to make him forget home? Forget all about me? We hadn't even made love, and I wasn't about to let someone else get what he wanted to give me. I couldn't let someone else love him. This man who I held tightly belonged to me. Marco was a part of me, having filled the void that was left by all the mess Cindy had made of my life.

By the time we got to my house and pulled in the driveway, my tears were replaced with a smile. I knew what I had to do and was willing to do it.

The minute the bike came to a stop and Marco turned off the engine, I said, "I'll go."

"What?" Marco got off the bike and pushed the helmet back, a big, wide smile on his face. Before I could say it again, he removed my helmet and kissed me so passionately, I thought I'd melt away to nothing. "You will never regret it. I'll make you happy, and I'll be there for you always."

I wasn't worried about money. I knew he had plenty of it. One time I looked in his bedroom drawer and it was loaded with cash. He didn't trust banks. No one knew, except me, that he'd inherited some money from his grandparents who'd lived in Florida. They'd left him so much that he didn't have to work. And he did make a few sound investments, which earned him even more.

Two weeks later, I graduated from high school, turning my red tassel from the right to the left. After standing in the long processional line to hear my name called out and listen to my family members cheer, I returned to my seat.

I looked over my shoulder and tapped Jimmy from math class and asked him to get Gabby's attention. She stopped talking long enough to look my way, and we both mouthed, "We made it," at the same time. Out of everybody else, I hated leaving her behind. Even worse, I hated that I couldn't tell her I would be going away with Marco. It wasn't that I didn't trust her not to rat on me. I just couldn't put her in the position of knowing all about it and lying when Aunt Debbie and Uncle Ed asked for specifics. This way, she wouldn't have to lie. There was only one reckless child in the house, and as of midnight, she would be moving on.

That night after everyone was in bed, I reached in the back of the closet and grabbed the two suitcases I had packed up. It wasn't everything by far, but it would be enough clothes to last me until Marco could take me shopping. I dressed quickly in jeans, a fitted tee, and a lightweight hoodie. Just as quickly, I slipped on a pair of socks and my navy-and-white sneakers. I'd worry about combing my hair later.

I looked around the room. I was all ready to go downstairs and out the door. I walked over to Gabby's side of the room. She was sleeping on her side, a slight smile on her lips. She must have been having a good dream. I wondered if it had anything to do with Vincent kissing her at the graduation party. As I stood there I thought about all the times she was there for me, and suddenly I felt an emergence of sadness. Before any other emotion could chime in, I pivoted and left the room, taking my sadness along with me.

I took the steps quickly, and fled the still darkness of the

Taylor household, taking the back door. Marco and I were going to California. Our plane would be taking off in five hours, and the airport was a two-hour drive away. I couldn't understand why and how he chose California, but a promise was a promise, and I'd promised him I'd go anywhere. We'd planned on getting married as soon as we got ourselves together. Then I'd let everybody know I was okay and happy being Mrs. Cassandra Brent. I was 18, and though it had only been for two minutes, could do as I pleased. Still, I wanted Aunt Debbie's blessing, or at least as much as she was able to give of it. I'd left a letter for Gabby, explaining and telling her the what, when, and how. She'd understand. She was my best friend and, more than anyone else, she would understand.

I turned one last time and looked at the house. Just then I saw myself on Uncle Ed's lap, and the next seconds, minutes, hours, days, months and years of it played in my mind in slow motion, it seemed.

I blinked back hot tears, and that's when I saw Gabby standing in our bedroom window, the curtain pulled back. Even from the distance, I could tell that she knew this wasn't just an overnight trip, partly because I stood in our driveway with two suitcases. She didn't budge, and neither could I. We just stared at each other, me waiting for her to turn away so my departing would be a little easier, and I believe she waited, hoping I would change my mind.

I dropped one suitcase to the ground and lifted one finger to my lips, asking her to keep this secret, at least until I was safely out of town and on my way. Little did I know, I was asking my best friend and cousin to keep yet another secret. I prayed right then as I picked up the other suitcase and walked to the end of the driveway, where Marco was waiting. What time wouldn't heal, distance would.

Chapter 2

Gabrielle

Twenty Years Later

I couldn't believe that I, Gabrielle Charay Taylor-Easton, had been pretending to be the adoring wife for so long, I had forgotten it was all just a front. I faulted myself only in part because the bottom line was, I couldn't help my upbringing.

Mom had taught me early in life that a wife should be loving, caring, and above all submissive, especially if she was fortunate enough to snag a good man. She told me more than once that good men were in high demand and hard to find. If you were lucky enough to hitch one that was employed in an occupation that could be listed on any legal document, and add to that a brother who provides for his family and showered them with materialistic perks, Mom along with every other African-American, or Caucasian woman for that matter, would consider that striking gold.

Mom didn't have to teach me about being submissive though, since I attentively watched her cater to my dad's every whim, God rest his soul, all because he was a provider. Didn't really matter what else he was. We were taken care of, and I guess, when the rubber meets the road, that's what matters most.

Now, in my case, if you add a regular tithe payer, position-holding church attendee, a good father, excellent son, and pillar in the community to Deborah Price-Taylor's priority list of husbandly attributes, Jeffrey Michael Easton would be the epitome of a decent man. Except that, with respect to him, there was some truth to the old adage about a wolf in sheep clothing.

The bonus for me was that Jeffrey was drop-dead handsome. The kind of handsome that would leave your mouth drier than the Sahara from the moment you set eyes on him. It would make you say, "Hmmm!" just watching his well defined body glide across the floor or have him just glance in your direction. He was fine. If I were to visually compare, he was a twist of Allen Payne, Boris Kodjoe, and LL Cool J.

As fine as he was, Jeffrey was just as blessed with an amazing singing voice, his velvety vocals emulating the sultry voice of Teddy Pendergrass. Yeah, he was talented in the vocal department, and once upon a time, he used his skills to serenade and woo me. I'd lose myself completely in him, and as hard as I tried not to, I was head over heels in love in no time. For that man, I would come completely undone in more ways than one.

We'd met in grad school and hit it off instantly. They say you can tell how a man will treat his wife by the way he treats his mother. His father had passed within a year of our meeting, and from that point on, I watched him assume the "responsible man" role in his mother's life, even though she was quite self-sufficient and more than capable of taking care of herself. Still, Jeffrey was always there for her, and they were not only mother and son, the two were friends.

I'd heard so many people say that things would go south after having kids. That wasn't us. The kids seemed to enhance what we had and made our love so much better. But somewhere along the line, and I can't exactly denote where, he stopped serenading me. Now, the only time I got a chance to enjoy his singing was from the closed bathroom door when he was in the shower, which, to me, was a sign that I was no longer the object of the musical notes that rolled so effort-lessly out of his mouth.

Our physical time together became abbreviated, our con-versation rushed, and the kiss out the door in the morning forgotten. I'd never say what was happening to us had any-thing to do with another woman. I could've been wrong, but I was willing to put up everything I had and could borrow to wager against that. So what was happening? Life, I'd say, and its demands.

Jeffrey went after everything life had to offer in a grand way. And who could leave out the roof over our heads. The Easton home was a beautiful two-story, cathedral ceiling, four-bedroom, two-bathroom house positioned on a well-mani-cured landscaped lot, accented with plenty of lighting. A flash from my past had made the extra lighting necessary, and he obliged with no hesitation.

It was complete with a three-car garage, in-ground pool with deck, glass-enclosed sunroom, and closed in with a white picket fence, which he said was for a little privacy, but I thought he was trying to create a visual storybook image.

We occupied about an acre of land and hadn't decided what to do with the additional two acres we'd purchased. All these extras that were added after our marriage were the ulti-mate ingredients for a good life, yet, unbeknownst to anyone, I had been praying desperately for the "happily ever after" to return.

Any outsider looking in would say that the only thing miss-ing was a dog, which I was on my way to pick up from the veterinarian. I smiled to myself because, frankly, I couldn't be-lieve how ironic the assigned task was, especially since every-one in the house was totally in love with the chow, except me.

The excitement of pet ownership was stolen from me early in life when Dad constantly turned down my request for get-ting a puppy. I'd drag him to the pet store whenever we went to the mall. Even though he agreed to carry me down to the store, we'd breeze through so quickly, with him pulling me along, I hardly had a chance to glance at the caged puppies that desired a home like mine. Whenever someone at church had a litter of puppies, they would mention it to my mom, only for her to come home excited with the possibility of finally making my dream of pet ownership come true, then have the balloon of hope shot down.

When Cassie came to live with us, she became a third voice to our begging efforts, yet that didn't change his mind. He claimed that neither of us was capable of handling all the responsibilities that went along with having a dog. That diminished the fire and took away the thrill of it totally. He himself was on the road so often, he didn't have time. Considering what I know now after years of being on the receiving end of what worked for him and what didn't, even if he had time, he still wouldn't have let a dog set foot in our house. How could I have thought that Ed Taylor would chance getting his alligator or spectator shoes licked by a canine, no matter how cute and how fond I was of said canine?

Jeffrey knew the childhood story well, and knew I didn't want a dog. But for the kids' sake and Jeffrey's, we were the proud owners of a dog, and I was conveniently assigned the task of being the designated doggy keeper and gofer.

So, here I was picking up Sable, a light brown furry ball of pure energy. I stood peeping over the counter waiting for a glimpse of Sable, to mentally gauge how hyper she was and to assess what our drive home would be like. When I didn't see her round the corner, I turned my attention back to the receptionist and waited for her to retrieve Sable's chart electronically.

Mentally, I was going over the rest of my to-do list for the day. Most people had the opportunity to wind down at the end of the workday, but I wasn't one of the lucky ones. For me 5:00 P.M. marked the beginning of the nightshift at the Easton plantation. Much like the slaves of old, I didn't get paid for the hard work I put in, nor were there breaks, time off, or any bonuses.

"Mrs. Easton, that will be one hundred fifty-five dollars."

I grimaced when the receptionist jolted me out of my thoughts. "For a couple of shots and a trim?" Half-joking, I added, "Next time I'll just get the shots and take my chances on trimming her myself. There has to be some how-to book I can get off the Internet. You know YouTube has a little of everything." I lifted my finger to help make the point.

Gloria was looking at me crazy and crossed-eyed for even bringing up the possibility. Obviously, she didn't know how serious I was. *How difficult could it be?*

"And mess up Sable's beautiful coat? Dr. Baker would have a fit." Gloria was smiling.

Even though I complained every visit, Sable was a regular customer and didn't miss an appointment. "Well, Dr. Baker can extend me a discount, and I'll be able to continue to afford Sable this luxury. Oh, by the way, can I get another supply of heartworm pills? I believe she has only one left."

"Sure. Since I've already totaled your bill for today, I'll put it on your account and add it to your next visit." Gloria turned toward an open cabinet behind her and pulled out a box of heartworm tablets. She opened the box then checked the side to make sure it was the proper dosage for Sable.

"Jeez! Thanks."

Gloria knew I wasn't trying to sound sarcastic and wasn't at all offended. In fact, she laughed at my reaction. I didn't see the humor, nor did I view the delay in payment as a break, but at least I wouldn't have to worry about the thirty dollars for a few months. I'd use my savings to treat myself to a trip to the nail salon.

"Okay, I'm outta here. Let me just grab Ms. Attitude."

I walked over to the door, and Gloria opened it from the other side and let a very excited Sable out. The minute the door opened, Sable charged out like she was auditioning for one of those dog food commercials.

I shouted, "Sable! Don't even think about acting wild. I'm not in the mood."

As if she understood every word, Sable sat down and tilted her head to the side.

"Right. Like you really understand and plan on acting like a normal dog." I connected her leash to her collar and tried to muster up the energy I knew I would need.

A quick good-bye to Gloria, and I was out the door, with Sable trying to run in front of me.

Racing back in the direction I just came from, I was more than fifteen minutes late picking up the kids. Turning my wrist slightly to check my watch to make sure the digital read-out in the car was correct, I sighed and said out loud, "Mom would chastise me and tell me my time management skills need some improvement." Forcing a smile, I wished she could tell me that. Since her stroke, she hadn't been able to say anything.

The speech therapist had such a difficult job at rehabilitating Mom, who was so headstrong, she'd sit in her wheelchair totally upright and regal and look out the window as if she wasn't interested in anything the therapist had to say, or teach her to say. I was grateful she was alive, don't get me wrong, but the state of her health wasn't much like living. Most people may have been able to deal with it, but Pastor Deborah Taylor was always a woman of many words.

Like all the other times before, thinking of my Mom's situation made me so solemn, and I felt so helpless. I smiled again. "She'd tell me to call on the name of the Lord more often." I didn't doubt that I needed to call on the Almighty, but Mom never understood, not even before she got sick, that I was doing the best I could. I wasn't like her. I couldn't juggle the affairs of my family, endure the trials and tribulations, work, and still act as if life was all glamorous and together, like she did. I just didn't have it like that, and I doubted whether it would happen for me just like that after all this time. She never understood that I was maximizing twenty-four hours like it was seventy-two, stuffing as much into it the way an overweight sister would force herself into her favorite two-sizes-too-small garment.

Jeff added to Mom's summation, always saying I was absentminded, never on time for anything, and didn't get done half the things that needed to be done. He said it so often, I had grown numb. Never mind that I was a working professional, a counselor at that.

It was my job eight hours a day, five days a week to listen to the issues of women, and based on what I'd learned in a bunch of textbooks and clinical studies, I could give them a well-thought out, reasonable, sensible, psychological diagnosis and go forth with a plan of action. Oftentimes the inside picture could look so bleak, dim, and depressing, moving on could seem impossible, but it was a necessary process that could make the difference between just existing or living life to the fullest. Occasionally, I'd fill in for one of the other counselors and deal with kids or a family, but my area of focus at the clinic was women, and I enjoyed what I did and wanted to believe that what I did gave others hope and, through the profession, made a difference.

I had an undergraduate and graduate degree in psychology and a dozen certificates on the wall that said I was good at what I did. From a young girl, I knew I wanted to help people feel better about themselves. When I decided to attend Virginia Commonwealth, I continued to be interested in helping people, but my mission became even more direct. I was determined to study hard and learn everything I could in the field, with the hopes of being able to assist patients in healing their minds and empowering them to reach beyond and outward. The latter came from my spiritual upbringing. I knew God had so much more in store for the lives of women. That may have sounded preachy, but what did anyone expect from me, I was a PK (preacher's kid), and periodically, that engrained thing spilled out of me without the wave of a white flag.

That's what I did for a living, which enabled me to contribute to all the things my husband felt we had to have. But, at the end of the day, once I placed my clinical jacket on the door hanger behind my office door, walked out of the Whitman Family Clinic, drove the distance to our home, stepped out of my Italian leather designer pumps, removed my power suit, and all the remnants that were a part of my outside makeup, I'd look into my bedroom mirror and come face to face with someone who was in need of the same type of therapy that I provided those that enlisted my services. With my personal affairs, I went from feeling it was my fault, to trying so hard to overcompensate for what I thought were my shortcomings. Many times I became physically sick; other times, well, I put it all away neat and tidy and pretended none of what I felt deep down existed. I would then resolve to be okay with it all for sanity sake and convince myself that if I was truly ever close to the danger zone, I'd know it. After all, I was a trained professional with an eye for acute disorders and problems, right?

The cell vibrated, reminding me I had forgotten to change the setting to a ring, "Hello." I didn't bother to look at the display to see who was calling me.

Zee's voice bellowed through the phone line. "Hey. You home yet?"

I adored Zee and appreciated so many things about her, loudness and all. She was the senior accountant for the clinic and had in fact recommended me for the counselor job when I decided to return to work after Jay started school. Zenith

Ray Gibson had it all together and was as beautiful as she was intelligent. Her short-cropped, auburn hair accented her lighter skin tone and hazel eyes, but despite her constant struggle to lose weight, she continued to tip the scale on the overweight side. She'd never been married, had no kids, and no love interest that I knew of. She went overboard telling everyone that she was content with her status and okay with her life just the way it was, but I knew better. Had she been, she wouldn't have been broadcasting it so often. She was my girl, and we were always there for one another.

It had actually been Cassie who started the rumor about Zee's real name, Zenith. They'd never cared for each other all that much and only tolerated each other's presence because of me. Cassie told everyone that Zee's mother named her only child after her best friend, a 25-inch floor model Zenith television set.

"No. Don't you remember me passing you in the hallway and telling you I had to pick up Sable from the vet?" I maneuvered past a car that slowed to make a turn at the last minute. "Now I'm on my way to pick up the kids."

"Oh, that's right. Gabby, sweetie, I don't mean to cause no trouble, but isn't his office closer to the vet? I mean, the last time I checked, it was like a few blocks away from the building where he works." She paused and asked me to hold a second.

I listened as she talked to someone at the gym.

"I'm just saying, wouldn't it make more sense for him to do the doggy pickup?"

"Yeah, but I had to do it." Zee was right and I had thought the very thing all the way to the vet and even that morning when he'd assigned me the task. "It doesn't matter. It's not a big deal." Her questioning only put me in a deeper state of wonderment. "Listen, I know you getting ready to work out. You do that, and I'll hit you later."

"Oh, okay." Zee spoke again. "Gabby, I'm just saying, you

can't do it all, despite you wanting to be the prototype for the ideal wife and mother."

I rolled my eyes, not at what she said, but because she was right. "Talk with you later."

This was the summation of my life story lately. Despite everything, my love for Jeffrey was still intact, and I took my vows seriously and honored the commitment we'd made to one another. Jeff, the ideal attentive boyfriend, fiancé, and husband back in the day, had promised me so much in the early years. Never in a thousand years would I have thought I'd end up hostage in a marriage.

I wouldn't call what we were experiencing a mountain, but it was, without question, a little molehill, a marital hiccup, certainly something we would overcome. That I knew. The reality check alerted me periodically that what we were currently in, offered me none of the security and love I had longed for, the one thing I'd craved for since I was a young girl.

To make matters worse, Jeff felt no bump at all when it came to our union. He wouldn't even entertain suggestions for us to rekindle the flame, to somehow find our way back to where we'd started. We'd wandered off the path of happiness, and I couldn't get us back on track all by myself. I spoke aloud again, "Asking him again will only irritate him and start an argument I'm just not up for."

Sable barked as if in agreement. I glanced up into the rearview mirror and watched her run from one side of the Explorer's cargo area to the other. "I know, girl. I've got to stop talking to myself." That had actually been the first time she'd barked since we pulled off. In fact, I had almost forgotten that she was in the truck with me.

Just as I settled down again to drive, I decided to listen to a little music. I reached for the radio to tune into the local gospel station when my cell phone blasted from inside my purse. "Okay, Sable, which one of my impatient children is about to rake me over the coals for being late?" They had definitely inherited Jeffrey's impatient gene trait, and could be as bad as him sometimes. I had the patience of Job and didn't mind waiting for just about anything. If it was something I really wanted, I was persistent, but I never grew irritated when I didn't get "instant."

Again Sable barked as I reached to answer the phone, never even bothering to look to see who it was interrupting me for the second time. "Hello."

"Gabby, I hope you picked up Sable." Jeffrey didn't bother to give me a warm greeting, nor did he give me a chance to respond before shouting out, "Where are you anyway?"

I should have reminded him that his office was around the corner from the vet, and so it would have made more sense for him to drive my car and pick Sable up. But then he wouldn't have been able to sport his Corvette.

I didn't trip when he decided six months ago to go out and buy a brand-new candy apple red Corvette, which I thought was a midlife-crisis purchase, a toy for a man trying to hold on to his youth. I had a newsflash for him—the youth was gone, just like much of his hair. I'd never voice that to him, although it felt good to think it. He'd be devastated if he knew it ran across my mind every time I looked at him. I knew it would definitely take a little hot air out of his "got-it-going-on" balloon.

I decided to call him by his nickname, which I never did, because he didn't like for people to shorten his birth name at all. He became Jeff when he pushed my emotional buttons way too hard.

"Jeff, my four o'clock patient went over their time a little, and I was late leaving the office. Then it took them a few minutes to get Sable settled. Now, I'm driving like a mad woman to pick up Alexis and Jay."

I pictured our children while he went on and on. I had

never called Jay by his given birth name, Jeffrey, or even Jeff. I thought it was cute fourteen years ago when I'd named him after his father. I had barely adjusted to being the mother of one, when exactly one year and one day after Alexis Da'jae Easton was born, my little Jay, Jeffrey Michael Easton, Jr., made his entrance. Jay was a smaller version of his father. The two were identical in complexion and features. His eyes were a piercing brown, and he towered me at six feet one and wore a size eleven in shoes.

With black shoulder-length hair, Alexis was a beautiful all-natural girl who didn't care about the extras. She usually styled her hair in a carefree ponytail or some low-maintenance hairdo and was done with it. Her body was filled out in all the right places, and for many of the young boys at her school, she was likely at the top of their interest list. Alexis' eyes were as piercing as her father's, but she was a smooth cocoa-brown like her mother, grandmother, and aunts.

Alexis and Jay were going through growing pains physically and hormonally, pleasant one moment and a ticking short fuse the next. I prayed it was just growing pains, and that they didn't end up being unpredictable emotional yo-yos. I considered it a blessing to have two healthy kids, despite their premature births and complications that lasted the first two months of their lives.

"Why didn't you cut your patient off? You knew you had to get to the vet and then pick up the kids?" Jeffrey breathed real hard. "I'll see you at home in an hour. Have dinner ready. Can you at least do that?" He hung up.

Just as I was about to throw the cell phone on the passenger seat, it rang again. I picked it up quickly and flipped it open. "What now?" I screamed into the small gadget.

"Mom, I was just wondering if you were almost here? We're standing in front of the recreation center. Alexis just got out of dance class, and I finished practicing thirty minutes ago."

I didn't answer right away.

"Mom, are you okay?"

"I'm sorry, Jay. I'm turning off Bennett Street now. I'll be there in a second."

I wiped my cheek, expecting the moistness of a tear that may have escaped beyond the wall, but it was sealed away, and I struggled my best to keep it that way. I didn't want them to sense that anything was wrong, so I did a little deep breathing and prayed for strength. This wasn't a time for things to get to me. Actually no time was the appropriate time, so I tucked everything back in the recesses of my mind and blinked a couple of times.

I needed to speed up my search for a therapist, but I didn't want to talk with anyone in my office, or anyone affiliated with our clinic. The last thing I needed was for someone to question my ability to deal with others' affairs, when I was struggling to juggle my own.

There wasn't really anyone I trusted, except Cassie. I smiled at the thought of her, and how much I still missed her.

Zee wasn't the one. She couldn't listen to anything I had to say without giving her opinion, usually a doom-and-gloom forecast. She wasn't a big fan of Jeffrey, to begin with, because she saw through what I worked hard to cover up, concerning me and him. She felt he was a dictator and had a huge ego that he needed to get over. She continuously said that he didn't support me enrolling in the Ph.D. program I was interested in because I would hold something that he didn't, giving me the upper hand.

And she was his worst nightmare. The mention of her name caused him to frown to the point that I thought the wrinkles would become permanent. He swore she was a walking, talking divorce advocate and couldn't keep a man because she was a man herself.

By the time I entered our black-and-white ultra modern kitchen, I was beyond exhausted. I dropped the keys on the countertop near the door and eyed the box of cereal on the island and the opened carton of soy milk. That meant I had at least thirty minutes to prepare a quick nutritious meal before Jay would announce his urgent need for food. Alexis was living off love these days, and even though I didn't have X-ray vision and could see up the steps and through the wall, I knew she was nestled on her bed with her cell phone pressed to her ear, talking to her boyfriend.

Sable finally calmed down in her designated corner of the garage after I fed her and placed fresh water in her dish. The corner was more like a mini-bedroom, since it included carpet, an extra large suede doggie bed, personalized food and water dishes, and two Wizard scented night lights plugged into the nearby outlets to keep her home smelling sweet.

I picked up the carton of milk and returned it to the door of the refrigerator. This provider of pet pickup service, errand person, and driver was about to put on her chef hat, all in a span of one hour. I looked at the clock positioned over the table and rubbed my forehead. I had to hurry. Jeffrey would be home soon, demanding everything from food, drink, ESPN, and the newspaper. The order sometimes changed, but the items almost always remained the same.

I was too tired to put one foot in front of the other and knew pulling off dinner wasn't going to be easy. I sat down at the breakfast nook and reached down to slip off one of my brown leather pumps. I rubbed the ball of my flesh-tone, nylon-covered foot and sighed.

The house phone rang before I could decide what to do next. I lifted the phone from the cradle on the first ring, trying to beat my kids to the punch. I didn't want them on the phone before they'd completed every assignment for every class and done one hour of required reading. "Hello."

"Gabby, dear, this is Ms. Emma." Her voice carried a deep Southern drawl and was easily recognizable. Every word she said was drawn out, and she held on to every syllable for dear life before it finally escaped out of her mouth.

Ms. Emma was one of my mother's oldest and dearest friends. Although she had a few medical problems of her own that restricted her from leaving the house, she was privy to all the neighborhood gossip.

I did appreciate her though. When Mom came home after her stroke, Ms. Emma volunteered to help me care for her and protested when I wanted to hire a nurse. She wasn't long in telling me that she herself was a retired registered nurse and had more experience than anyone I could bring in, that no one could give her Deborah the bedside attention and love that she could. I couldn't deny that, so that very week, we moved her into my Mom's home, and she rented her house out to one of her cousins. With her daughter living away, and her being a widow for fifteen years, there was no other family in the area, except her adopted family—me, Cassie, and Mom.

"Hey, Ms. Emma. Is Mom okay?" I quizzed quickly. This was a little early for her nightly call. My evening pattern usually included a trip to Mom's, to make sure they had whatever they needed, and to chat with them about any and everything.

"Well, sweetie, Jamie called this morning, and they going to induce labor day after tomorrow. She argued that I didn't need to come right away to help, but I'm thinking that I need to be there as soon as possible. You know what I'm saying?"

"Oh, my. She's not due for another three weeks, right?"

I was trying to cover up my emotion, but I couldn't believe that this was happening to me. What was I supposed to do now? My mind raced a mile a minute, and I began to hyperventilate. It wasn't so much because I minded caring for my mother, it was just that Jeffrey was going to blow his lid when I told him that I would have to stay there or bring Mom into our home.

"Yes, that's right, but she's having some complications. She keep saying she don't need her Momma, but you know she'd be a lot better off with me right there to help out and do what I can do. I sure hate to run out on Debbie, but she nodded that she understood and gestured that I go."

"Mom's right. You should. I understand perfectly." I closed my eyes tight and opened them slowly, hoping for this to be a dream. "Well, let me talk to Jeffrey and figure out how we're going to work it out. I guess I can take off a few days until we get everything organized and together."

"Jeffrey should have no problem with this. See what I'm saying? You girls need to worry less about your men folk and more about what matters. That's Jamie's problem—worrying about taking care of Eric, while she should be worrying about those babies. She needs all her energy. And there you go worrying about what Jeffrey wants to do." She sucked her teeth.

I could imagine the look on Ms. Emma's face. "I know, Ms. Emma. Listen, let me get my thoughts together, and I'll call you back in a while. I haven't started dinner yet. Listen, I'll work it out, don't you worry. I love you, and tell Momma I love her. Okay?"

"Okay, sweetness. I'll chat with you later."

The phone line went dead, but instead of returning the phone to the cradle, I held it. I decided to take a shortcut. I called out for pizza and confirmed how long it would take for the delivery person to arrive.

While I waited, I threw together a salad to balance our nutritional needs as I buzzed around the kitchen and busied myself with chores, my overloaded thoughts keeping me company. After Jeffrey ate, read the paper, and watched a little television, I would talk to him about Momma.

Jay came downstairs beating on the wall nosily. He looked around the kitchen and toward the range. "Mom, what's for dinner?"

"Pizza with grilled chicken, mushrooms, and extra cheese, buffalo wings, and a salad."

"Cool." Hearing the scratching noise at the garage door, he walked past me and patted my shoulder. "I'll take Sable out."

"Why?" I chuckled. He usually debated five minutes at least before budging to take Sable out. "It must have something to do with me ordering your favorite pizza."

"You're right, and the wings are a plus. You are the woman." Jay laughed, drumming the counter all the way to the door.

I watched him open and close the door to the garage and smiled. Since he'd started drum lessons a couple of months ago, everything in sight became an instrument for him to practice on. I went to the sink and looked out toward the backyard.

I thought about Mom. I had to come up with something. Then it hit me. There was one person who could possibly help me. I just hoped she wouldn't turn me down flat, or decide not to return my call, as she so often did.

It was such a long shot, and I probably had no right to ask something this big. Mom was my responsibility, I knew that, but if I could get a little assistance for a couple of weeks, I'd be able to plan the "what next." I knew the number by heart because I dialed it almost every other week. Occasionally, I'd talk to the answering machine; other times I'd hang up after a few rings, accepting that reaching out was useless.

I retrieved my cell phone from my purse and dialed before I changed my mind.

"Hello, Cassie."

Chapter 3

Cassandra

"What's your next move?" Ginger asked, full of concern. "I mean, I know all of this is happening pretty fast, but please tell me you have a plan B."

A light breeze stirred through the nearby trees. Trees were a hot commodity in California, and whenever I got the opportunity to enjoy its offerings, I was reminded of home.

Ginger had invited me to lunch in hopes of cheering me up. I had no idea what she had in mind was a chili dog, chips, and Coke from the vendor cart outside the hospital. The seating was just as creative, a park bench across the street.

Love her heart. I couldn't be upset. She only had an hour for lunch and chose to spend it with me, knowing I wasn't in the best of moods and that my mind was crowded with the what next of my life.

"You know me. I wouldn't be caught midstream without a plan B. I learned that lesson the hard way, but nonetheless it was a lesson well learned."

"Well, Lilly said that the layoff shouldn't last long. She even asked me to have you call her." Ginger bowed her head in a prayer of thanks and took a big bite of her chili dog and chewed a few times. She added, "There's a few private-duty opportunities, and she wanted you to contact the agency today. I think she already told them about you, and recommended you highly."

I appreciated Ginger being the messenger, but how could I trust anything that Lilly offered? She had been the one to hand me and two other nurses over on a silver platter. Instead of cutting in some other areas, she decided to give up three staff members, all for the bottom line.

I wasn't supposed to know the details, but Sonya, who worked in Human Resources, made it a point of telling me just enough to know that I was stabbed in the back. All the while my supervisor was smiling in my face. Sure, the song and dance was supposed to make me feel so invaluable, and somehow comforted with the way she fought the decision from the higher-ups. Please. She gave us up at the first sit-down meeting regarding the departmental budget, all so she could keep the latest equipment on her floor. Like going down or up a floor would hinder our services. So, a month ago, I joined the ranks of the unemployed.

"I have some money saved. What's a girl to do without some mad money?"

"One better than me. Chile, if they decide to give me my walking papers on a pink color slip, I'm going to be carless and homeless. I don't save nothing, and I live well above my means." She rolled her eyes. "I upset myself."

"Don't. It takes discipline. It wasn't always this way for me. As I said, I had to learn some hard lessons. I wouldn't wish my method of coming to the realization that I needed to always have a security blanket on anyone."

"Just the same, you have it more together than most," Ginger said.

"Thanks for that. I don't think I'm going to check out the private duty gig though." I wiped my mouth with a napkin and took a sip from the Coke can.

"Why? You have something else going on?" Ginger looked me in the face without blinking.

"I may be going back home for a few months."

I'd been thinking about it since I'd received the voice mail from Gabby a couple of days ago. It wasn't until last night that I decided to call her back. After exchanging pleasantries, and me telling her how well I was doing with my own private duty company, I listened to her blow her horn about work and her wonderful family. That's why I beat her to the punch. I didn't want her to think that my life was nothing. I felt some regret, though, for coming out and lying to her when I knew that sharing her update wasn't her way of bragging. In fact, I think she was just excited to be sharing her world with me after so much time had gone by.

What was clear from Gabby was that Aunt Debbie need-ed me. I didn't even know she had a stroke. In my stupidity whenever Gabby left a message, I listened to see if anything was earth-shattering or urgent, and once I made the determi-nation it wasn't, I never returned the calls.

At first, even though I didn't understand why, I wanted to punish them for what happened to me. I wanted to somehow connect losing Cindy to them, although there were no real dots to connect there. After a few years, I got over that, but by then, none of what Marco promised happened, and I was too embarrassed to keep in touch with them. The calls between me and them in the beginning were brief, and each ended with a reminder that I could always come home. I kept telling myself that I'd come clean, but months turned into years, and I was still pretending to be living it up in Oakland, California, in the lap of luxury, I might add.

There had been no luxury from the time we stepped off the plane. We lived a modest life in the projects, something I was not even remotely used to. Marco had no inheritance, and the money he did have from his true occupation dwindled quickly from all the partying and drinking he did. To sup-port us, I got a job as a receptionist at the hospital and waited tables at Red Lobster at night. By then Marco was in and out, but mostly out. It was up to me to make my life in a place that was cold, large, and unfamiliar.

Many times I'd packed up with the intention of heading back home. Once, I made it all the way to the bus station, got on the bus, and was a whole state away from Oakland, but I returned, because pride wouldn't let me. Somewhere along the line, determination fueled me to drive forward.

When the hospital promoted me to a secretarial position, which paid a lot more, I stopped waiting tables and started taking classes at the nearby university. The hospital paid for the college course, so I saw no reason why I shouldn't enroll. Nothing else had worked out the way I'd planned, but this would be one thing I could try to make happen. I worked every day and overtime whenever I could, and at night I went to school. I made a year-round commitment to my education, and somehow I graduated and went from answering phones, typing, and filing in the billing office to a full-time position as a floor nurse in the geriatric unit.

Once I graduated and received a signing bonus, Marco decided to be out more than in, since it looked like I could make it on my own. He finally landed a job that he simply loved—being a drug dealer—, which gave him all the attention he wanted and positioned him to be the big boss man he always wanted to be.

We moved from the projects and, with my credit in decent order, bought a condo. Just when it seemed like things were going well between us and we were on our way to getting married per his daily reminder, we fell apart. He said I wasn't supportive of his status as a rising kingpin, so he left me.

After letting him come back to my bed more times than I should have, I shut him out physically. The progress of going from madly in love and living with Marco to him being in and out, his upgrade to kingpin, and being told that he would stop dealing once he made some real money, the promises and disappointments, it all took twenty good years out of my life. It had been twenty years since I'd left Virginia's Eastern Shore, and the first time that I'd even seriously considered going back.

Except, Marco still kept his place in my heart, and while we couldn't be together forever, occasionally I'd call him. When he called, I listened, not wanting to tell him how I craved him, how he was still so much a part of me. That he could never know. That would have made me a fool, and I couldn't play that role for a lifetime.

I'd dated a time or two and spent time with this one guy who swore we were soul mates, but I just wasn't on the same page and didn't think it was fair to have him believe that I believed in an "us." Marco Brent was the only man I had ever loved and the reason why my life changed.

"Are you sure you want to do that?"

Ginger didn't know much about my life back home. Being privy to my on-again, off-again relationship with Marco was no secret, but back home was back home, sealed off from everything else.

"It's not really wanting to," I told her. "It's more that I need to. Besides, the chance to go back is actually coming at a good time. My savings won't last forever, and I would be just beating the pavement to find another job." I placed the paper from the hot dog in the empty chip bag. "This will give me a chance to beef up my resume and come back fresh."

Everything I said made sense, like a well thought-out plan. I just couldn't figure out when all of it started making sense to me.

"It does sound like a plan. I'm just going to miss you." Ginger stood up and looked at her watch. "Time for me to hit the clock."

"I know. Well, I do have a question." I stood up.

Ginger smiled. "Sure. Whatever you need."

"I know your lease is almost up and you are looking for a place. I'd like you to sublet my place."

"What? Really?" Ginger started smiling.

I had been her apartment-hunting buddy, and the places she had looked at were not half as nice as my condo, and none of them had the amenities that were included in what I was offering her.

"There is only one catch."

"Whatever it is, I'm sure we can work it out."

"I just need to keep my things in one of the guest rooms, and if I come back before we agree leasewise, I can bunk with you."

"Deal."

Instead of shaking on the deal, we hugged.

"Now I have a question."

"Whatever it is, I'm sure we can work it out." I laughed, mimicking what she'd said just seconds ago.

"Can I keep your furniture? My furniture is not nearly nice enough to put in your place, and besides, I only have a few odd pieces. I'll use my bedroom stuff because that's all I have that's new, but if I could use the rest, it would be great."

"Of course. That's not a problem." I was relieved that I wouldn't have to find someone to sublease my place, and even more relieved I wouldn't have to pack all my stuff up and put it in storage. That would have taken forever, and I only had a few days before I told Gabby I'd be home.

We said our good-byes, and I sat back down on the park bench. I was in no real rush now, since I only had a little packing to do. There were some other loose ends I needed to tie up, but for right now, I needed to let it sink in.

I leaned my head back against the bench and watched the trees move from side to side slightly in the light breeze.

I looked up at the sky and watched as the clouds joined and moved apart from one another.

There was a mixture of anxiety and anticipation as I thought about going back. Uncle Ed had passed fifteen years ago from a heart attack in the bed of another woman. What a blow that had to be for Aunt Debbie. In life he hadn't been loyal, and even in death he went out as Slick Taylor. From what Gabby told me in a long letter, the lady was married, and to avoid the whole ugly mess it could have created, she called some of my uncle's friends to move his body from her house and place him in his truck, a distance away from where she lived. But the best-laid plans don't always go well, and Aunt Debbie found out, and so did the lady's husband. Aunt Debbie ended up counseling the couple, and encouraged them to stay together.

That was much more grace and mercy than I would have extended, but then that was Aunt Debbie. I thought it would be hard to tell her that I couldn't come to the funeral because of work, but before I could go into all of that, she stopped me and told me it was so far, and that she understood. Attending the funeral of the man who helped raised me should have been something I didn't even have to debate, but then there was the secret, and not enough time had passed for me to face him again, living or dead. But now, after all this time I was going home.

Chapter 4

Gabrielle

I pulled my cinnamon red Ford Explorer into the parking garage and sucked my teeth for being later than usual. The parking lot next to the clinic was full to capacity and I would have to pay the daily rate. My routine of being one of the early and prompt ones, arriving forty-five minutes before I was due at work, went out the window this morning. No matter how I tried to maneuver, nothing went as planned. Murphy's Law had been in full effect, and I knew, in all likelihood, the rest of the day wouldn't yield a great improvement. I circled around one more time on the lower level to see if I had missed a spot when I noticed Janice waving at me. Every place of business, be it private or public sector, big or small, had a busybody, that one person who knew everyone's business and shared everything she or he learned with anyone who cared to listen. Janice Wilson was that person at Whitman Family Clinic.

I tried to deal with her cordially, but even that was a challenge. She made me want to cast what I considered my best qualities—being pleasant, upbeat, and jovial—in the sea and show her the ghetto side. I wanted to believe that she meant well, and since we worked at the same place for so long, I knew she possessed a heart of gold, but she just couldn't keep her nose out of other people's business, a hazard for those in the health profession, and especially for someone in the medical records departments who had access to all of our patients' medical information.

Almost every person has several sides and different layers of themselves, and Janice was no different. She currently cared for four foster kids. She treated them like they were her own and talked about them endlessly. Some people assumed the responsibility of being a foster parent only for the money, but Janice went out of her way to ensure that her kids had every advantage and all the support they needed to overcome the circumstances that had rendered them wards of the state.

They say opposites attract, and Oliver Wilson was the complete opposite of Janice. At every company gathering or whenever he came down to the clinic, he hardly opened his mouth.

After maneuvering my truck carefully between a black Camry and an older model Nissan Sentra, I busied myself with gathering my lunch bag, shoulder tote, and purse. I didn't even notice that Janice was standing at the elevator waiting for me until I closed the truck door.

"Good morning, Janice. How are you today?"

"Girl, you're usually here before now and already in your office ready to start the day. Don't tell me you've finally gotten tired of getting here early and having Terry waltz in any time she pleases." Janice stood at an angle, making sure she didn't miss my expression coming out of my mouth concerning one of the other counselors I worked with.

It wasn't my concern that Terry adjusted her hours, especially since I wasn't the one signing her paycheck. For the record, though, Janice had put her foot in her mouth again. Terry made early-morning visits to the juvenile facility before she reported to the clinic, but obviously Janice didn't catch that on the Whitman grapevine.

"I'm just a little later than usual today. It was crazy around my house this morning. No one wanted to get up, and then when they did, they moved with all the speed of a snail."

I had carefully chosen my words, since I knew part, if not all, of my reply would be told at the watercooler and coffee corner before noon. I was still paused at the part where she'd just turned Terry's lateness into something that should concern me. They were daily lunch buddies and, I thought, very good friends, but then again, why should I have been shocked? That's how Janice rolled. The girl had no loyalty, and her truth was always clouded or colorized to the point of being unrecognizable. Sad.

As we walked in unison toward the office, she said, "Gabrielle, you need to put Ms. Terry in her place. If you don't start saying something, she's going to continue to take advantage of you and have you covering her patients when she's late in the morning. You know she's been telling everyone that your marriage is in trouble."

"What?" I stopped and peeped at her over my sunglasses. I couldn't help raising my voice a couple of octaves. This was Janice, but still I didn't want a rumor like that going around, even if she'd just created the story on her own. I couldn't see Terry saying anything like that about me. "You can't be serious."

"She told Sonya that you called Craven and Thompson earlier this week to make an appointment." Janice paused then added, "I told Sonya that Terry should mind her business. If you want to get a divorce, it's nobody's business but your own. After all, nobody should have to live with someone who doesn't love them."

Janice was looking dead at me, waiting to see how I was going to respond to this outrageous gossip. She may not have started it, but she was helping to spread it. She, of course, would never own up to her role, and was sure to add my outburst to fan the flame.

"Look, Janice, I don't know how all this started, but my marriage is just fine. And for those people who have nothing better to do than eavesdrop on my phone calls, tell them to make sure they stand beside my door long enough to get the whole story. I won't entertain it, but think about this. My patients are women, and a few of them are in the middle of litigation." I swung the door open to our building. "Jeez! I can't believe you guys."

"Girl, I can't either. I'm glad I said something, so you know it wasn't me. I was telling them that you and Jeffrey are the happiest couple I know. And you know, girl, he's always doing nice things for you, and he loves those kids too much to leave them, no matter what."

When we reached my office, I pulled out my keys from my purse to open the door. "I'm sure you told them that." I looked her directly in the eyes, daring her to say another word or utter one more statement that bordered a lie. "I appreciate that, Janice. Now I'm going to get ready for a very busy day. I suggest you do the same. You know how Fridays can be."

She didn't say a word but walked away as if she was offended that I'd responded the way I did.

"What did she think I was going to say?" I said out loud, stomping around the office in anger. I opened my blinds slightly and turned on my Gateway computer. I removed my navy blazer and reached for my clinical jacket, putting my blazer where it had been hanging.

"Keep right on talking about me and my personal life. I don't even care. Sticks and stones." I walked in front of my desk, my arms folded.

Just then Zenith knocked on my door and proceeded to come in. "Dag! You got to stop talking to yourself."

"I know, but I am so pissed."

I walked around my oak desk. Management definitely didn't pour a lot of money in the office furniture budget, which I'd altered by adding a lot of personal pieces, including wall paintings, decorative lamps, and wicker baskets with floral arrangements. I even went so far as to purchase two beautiful side chairs from Ikea, which surrounded a small oak conversation table I'd picked up from a yard sale. With the help of Jeffrey, I was able to re-do it to near peak condition. The smell of jasmine and lilac flowed through the room from the strategically placed diffusers and the Yankee candle electric unit.

I touched a few keys on the keyboard and waited for the computer to wake up.

"Tell Momma Zee all your problems." She chuckled, knowing she sounded like one of those psychics on late-night TV.

"I walked in with Janice. Need I say more." I leaned back in my chair and drummed my desk with my manicured nails. *Dag! Jay was rubbing off on me.*

"Not a word. If you weren't Pastor Taylor's daughter and raised right, you'd probably be cursing instead of using nice, heaven-bound words." Zenith sat down in one of the chairs positioned in the corner of my office. "Me myself, I would have cursed the trick out and been done with it."

"Oh, Zee, that wasn't nice." I giggled while pulling up my schedule for the day.

"I'm sure what she said wasn't nice." Zee stretched her leg out and looked down at her right shoe. She was dressed in a simple black wrap dress with off black hose and low heel pumps. Her hair was shiny and looked freshly twisted. "I can go check her," she said, "but I'm sure you want me to just go straight to my office and mind my business, the same way she should be minding hers." Zee stood up and removed the schedule I had just printed from my hand, likely checking to see what my day looked like. She was always getting on me about jamming too many appointments in and not leaving enough time to have lunch or take a few breaks between appointments and preparing treatment plans and notes.

"You are right on both counts." Reaching for the paper she was returning, I opened my Day-Timer and glanced over that schedule to see if it matched what I had printed out. "The long and short of it, she was saying that Terry is telling everyone I was on the phone talking to a divorce attorney."

"That's not strange. Gosh, half of your patients are probably getting a divorce or thinking of getting one."

"They are saying I made the call for me, myself, and I." I leaned back and waited for Zee to respond to that one.

"Oh, they went too far. I could say that because I've got time vested in our friendship, and God knows I'm not happy with our marital relationship. And I say *our* because I consider myself in it too, but I'm not standing for anyone else spreading lies about your marriage."

"You are crazy." I didn't correct her because it was no use, and on top of that, she really believed she had as much say as I did about my marriage.

"You need to report Terry. If she is outside your door listening to your conversations and twisting stories, or heck, even telling it straight, she shouldn't. As a counselor she knows that. I suggest you share this little tidbit with Dr. Johns. She'd love to know. Isn't there like a doctor to doctor confidentiality creed, the same as doctor/patient?"

"It goes without saying, but I don't want anyone to get in trouble." I picked up a pen and started drawing circles on a pad.

"Why should you care? They don't. I'm sure they are already packing around the cooler to talk about your breakup." Zee was now walking in front of my desk, her arms folded, much like I had done when I'd first walked in.

"Girl, sit down. You're making me dizzy. And, for the record, you're right. I wish I could say I didn't think Terry is responsible for spreading this rumor, but I remember the call to Craven and Thompson, and just as I was hanging up, she'd walked in my office asking me about a code."

I went back mentally to a few days ago and remembered

how she instantly walked in the door the minute I hung up the phone, as if she had been outside waiting for the telephone conversation to be over. I hadn't closed the door behind my last patient because I was expecting someone right after her, and I saw no reason to get up twice. Even when I didn't have a patient in with me, my door was always cracked, unless I was working on a report. The thought of one of my colleagues eavesdropping and then sharing it with others was, in a word, wrong.

"That's close enough for me. Let's go see Dr. Johns." Zee walked toward the door and turned to me. "Are you coming, or do you want me to tell it for you?"

Dr. Candi Johns was the clinic's administrator. Our staff was small enough that she interacted with each of us.

"Girl, I don't need you to tell it for me. I'll call Dr. Johns and ask if I can discuss something with her later. Right now, I'm going to look over my notes for my nine o'clock appointment, and you, my sweet, are going upstairs to your office and keep this clinic in the black."

"Please. That's not a major challenge. You guys are raking in dough. There's a lot of mentally sick people out there."

"Don't put it that way, Zee. These people just need to talk through their issues and deal with their problems head-on."

"I say the end result is, I'm busy counting and balancing. It all works for me. Chat with you later." She started to walk out the door and turned around again. "Hey, we on for lunch?"

"I brought mine, but we can eat together if you want." I was ready to start my day and ready for Zee to go about her business and chat with me later.

"Sure. I'll order something you like, just in case you decide not to eat what you brought. I've never been one for leftovers."

"I have no problem with leftovers. Speak for yourself. Just call me when you're ready to break."

Once the door was closed, I relaxed and focused on the schedule in front of me. I couldn't allow the rumors to get under my skin.

Dr. Johns wasn't really impressed with Terry, who wasn't exactly the model employee. In fact, almost all of her patients, after a few sessions, asked to be placed with another counselor. Ironically, Dr. Johns had asked me for advice regarding the constant complaints about Terry, both from staff and patients. Being an advocate for second chances, I suggested she just give her a warning and talk to her. I was sure Terry would do better, once she was made aware that she wasn't conducting herself the way the company expected her to.

I just didn't want to believe she would listen in on my conversation, be it business or personal. But there was no other way anyone would have known I had called Craven and Thompson to make an appointment. I wanted to ask the firm to allow my report as findings in one of my patients' divorce hearings. Still, I wondered if I had enough evidence to support my going to Dr. Johns. I decided I'd think about it a while before making a decision. After all, what's done in the dark, or around the corner in this case, would come to light.

"Girl, are you going to eat the rest of that spaghetti?" Zee popped the last of my garlic bread in her mouth. For someone who didn't like leftovers, she'd been picking in my dish from the time I took it out of the microwave.

"What? Oh, yeah, go ahead. I'm full." I pushed the rest of the spaghetti over to her and folded my hands in front of me. "I want to ask you a question." I paused for her to encourage me to continue.

Zee's encouragement came as she chewed. "I knew something was on your mind. You haven't said much all morning, and you didn't even bother to comment about me eating your leftovers." She wiped her mouth with the napkin she removed from her lap and placed it over the plate I'd pushed toward her. I could tell she wanted to polish off the rest of it.

"Thanks. You just stopped me from overeating and paying the price later. I've been trying to cut back."

Zee was my friend, and I never wanted to hurt her feelings, but she had already entered the overeating zone, after polishing off a large cheese steak, large fries, a piece of garlic bread, half a dish of spaghetti, and chasing it down with a 24-oz. Diet Dr. Pepper.

"I'm going to be taking a few days off next week."

"Oh, okay. Are you doing some work around the house, or going someplace?" she quizzed, a puzzled look on her face.

"They're planning to induce Jamie's labor early, and Ms. Emma is going to be with her." I got up and went to the corner of Zee's office and retrieved a bottle of water from her mini-fridge. "So I'll need to stay with Mom until Cassie gets here."

"Cassie? Peachy. She comes to visit after all these years. What's it been, twenty, thirty years?"

Zee, even though she grew up with us, wasn't a big fan of Cassandra. I always knew it had nothing to do with Cassie offending her, but more because she wanted to be my number one friend. I remember Cassie had just moved into my house, leaving very little space for her. Prior to that, she was my daily playmate because she lived two houses down the street from me. I didn't even bother to tell Zee then that Cassie was always my best friend even before she'd moved in with us. Cassie and I were the two peas, but Zee was the third *amigo*. As a result, their relationship was strained.

"Don't be funny, Zee. Cassie has been gone a while, but it hasn't been thirty years." I removed the cap off the bottle of water and held it while I took a sip. It was twenty years, but I wasn't going to acknowledge for her benefit the exact time frame. "I asked her to come and help me care for Mom while Ms. Emma is gone."

"I would have helped you out. You know that." Zee got up from the small round table in the corner of her office and threw the remainder of the food away.

"I knew you would have, but neither of us has the training Cassie has. Besides, she is family."

Zee turned around. "What am I?"

"I mean, so are you, but I'm just saying, Mom would love to have Cassie come and care for her, and as I said, nursing is her field, and she is specifically trained in the care of older people."

"And you have that, on whose authority? Hers?" Zee rolled her eyes. "Please. She probably wants to come home because the well has finally run dry, or Marco has. The getaway was doomed the minute he paddled the boat to Cali with her in tow. It's more because of that than Aunt Debbie needing her assistance, and you getting up the nerve to ask her to come. You can beat that."

"Look, I'm not having this conversation with you, so don't waste your time by insulting Cassie, or me for that matter. She is like my sister. You know that, Zee. I've asked her to help me, and that's the end of the story. Now, she'll be here Monday afternoon. You will be around each other, I'm sure, so all I'm asking is that you leave your fangs and claws at the door." I was a little more than warm under the collar at her verbal assault on Cassie and was holding my breath. Just because Cassie wasn't here or because she hadn't been home in twenty years didn't mean that I would let anyone talk about her. Not even Zee, as much as I cared for her.

"I got it, Gabby. After all these years, you're still defending her. Lord knows, she doesn't deserve your loyalty."

"Stop! That's enough! I love you like a sister, you know

that, but Cassie is my blood, and regardless of what you think you know, there's so much more you don't know."

I got up from the table and walked out before she had a chance to reply. I was hoping she would adjust and get over Cassie's return.

My conversation with Cassie after all these years had been civil, and what I heard in her voice, I hadn't heard in a long time. It took a little persuading, but she was willing to come, and for that I was grateful. I was going to get everything ready for her, including checking Zee's attitude, before her plane touched down on the East Coast. If all went well, my best friend wouldn't be returning to Oakland, she would be coming home to stay.

Chapter 5

Cassandra

Who says it never rains in Southern California? It had been raining for the past five days. Just when one of the popular meteorologists from one of the local television station affiliates announced in the wee hours of the morning that the day's forecast would be a sharp contrast from the past week, that we would be experiencing sunny skies and warm temperatures, Mother Nature did a switch. Just as we were pulling away from my condo, the sky opened up and released huge drops of rain.

I'd never relied on weather reports all that much. Sure, many times they were right on the money, but every now and then, they'd be so far off, it even made folk like me carry an umbrella when there wasn't a cloud in the sky.

I wasn't much for good-byes or sentimental expressions of any kind, so I called a cab instead of having Ginger drive me to the airport. She argued and went on and on, disagreeing with my reasoning that it was out of her way, and much too early to make the drive after she'd just walked in from pulling a double shift.

I hadn't allowed many people to penetrate my makeshift wall of defense since coming to California. In fact, from the time I'd stepped off the plane, I didn't want to know or get attached to anyone. I told myself, all I needed was Marco, and it stayed that way. I knew people and interacted with them easily. I mean, I wasn't a total recluse or anything close to it.

I just had a limit as to how close people got to me. *Hi. How are you? What's new? Take care,* and *Have a nice day* were easy exchanges and didn't require any real connection. At least, that's the way it was in the beginning.

When Marco started being out more than in, I become more of an introvert, and by the time he left me totally, I was a certified loner. I didn't want anyone in my inner circle of three, the three being me, myself, and I.

Ginger had been one to see beyond the wall, and instead of walking away and labeling me difficult and one to leave alone, she'd talk to me even when I didn't readily answer or act as if I cared to answer. Whenever we were on the same shift, she'd talk and talk, determined to chisel away the bitterness, which I put on, like my colorful nurse's smock. The world didn't owe me anything, and that wasn't my rationale. I was determined, though, not to place myself in a position to expect anything either.

One day she left a note on my clipboard telling me she was sorry I was unhappy, that I needed to get over it and stop letting it eat away at me. For a while, I ignored and avoided her, thinking, *Who does she think she is, all up in my business? And how does she know something is eating away at me?* Then it came to me weeks later that she had witnessed me swallowing antacids like they were candy. She'd obviously concluded that my stomach ailment had nothing to do with heartburn or indigestion. I admired that she cared enough to even say anything, and that she was observant. She reminded me of Gabby, caring about people even when they didn't deserve it. From that point on, she became the only person in California I could call a friend.

I had thought about taking a cheaper, slower mode of transportation, i.e. Greyhound, but I would have never gotten to the Eastern Shore by the date I told Gabby I would be there. Not to mention, I wasn't exactly thrilled about the prospect of busing it. Gabby had mentioned that she would pay me for caring for Aunt Debbie, but how could I accept money to care for a woman who helped raise me after Cindy died? And, besides, I was supposed to own a profitable private-duty nursing agency, which didn't exactly equate to being broke as a joke. When I'd checked the price of a ticket home, I grimaced and turned off the computer, the ticket price was going to dip into my savings big time, but somehow I'd make it work. I wasn't worried about needing a lot once I was there. After all, back home wasn't exactly a high-cost area, and God knows, when I left, there wasn't that much going on in terms of living. Things change, of course. I knew that. I just didn't think that it was screaming excitement, fast pace, or anything close.

The day after I talked with Gabby, before I could make my own arrangements, I received an electronic ticket from the airline via e-mail, all paid for. Of course, I immediately called to save face, informing her I was more than able to pay my own way, but she wouldn't hear of it, explaining that I was doing her a favor. I felt bad listening to her refer to it as a favor. I was going to care for the woman who had cared for me when I had no one else. I didn't say that to Gabby though. I just prayed that, somewhere between my arrival and departure, I'd be able to deal with my yesteryears and heal.

The back of the cab was warm. In fact, it felt like the air conditioning wasn't working. I leaned forward and ask the cabbie to turn it up.

The driver, who looked like a throwback from the '70s, with his long, greasy-looking hair pulled back in a ponytail, and leather vest over a white T-shirt, said, "Sure, honey. I'll try to crank it up, but I've been having trouble with it all week."

I leaned back and felt a little relief after a few minutes. I went over everything I had done in the last two days, making sure I hadn't left anything out. With all my business taken care of, and everything major forwarded to Aunt Debbie's address, I was pretty much ready to travel. I knew I was coming back and had no intentions of residing in the backwoods country town I grew up in. Yet, many of the last-minute errands I took care of had a feel of finality I couldn't explain or make sense of.

There was one thing I had to do before I left California, and it had nothing to do with me moving away temporarily. It was long overdue, and something I needed to do if I was going to finally move on. This layoff was a wake-up call and afforded me the chance to see life through different color lenses. Many times, the most drastic change in your life can cause you to honestly reflect and bring order to your state of affairs.

Before I changed my mind, I opened my cell phone address book and clicked down to his name and pressed talk. I took several deep breaths, thinking that maybe I'd be talking to his voice mail, since it took forever for him to answer.

"Hello." His voice sounded deep and groggy, like he was still sleeping.

I glanced at my watch. *Dag!* It wasn't eight o'clock yet. Marco wasn't an early-morning person. He'd probably just climbed in bed, and quite likely wasn't alone. The idea of someone laying there with him naked after making passionate love to him caused my stomach to flip. Maybe this was a bad idea, but he was on the line now, and my number would show up.

"Marco, this is Cassandra."

"What's up, baby girl?"

No matter how many times he'd walked out, and even when I swore it was his last time, he'd call me baby girl, as if it was okay to remain in that intimate space with me.

"I need to talk to you." I watched the rain glide down the window.

"Go on. I'm listening to you."

"No, it has to be in person. But here's the thing. I can't come over because I don't have my car, so you'll have to meet me at the airport."

"The airport? What? You going someplace or just coming back?" he asked, sounding more alert now.

Marco was no longer the man in my life, but I knew he was aware of my every move. He'd told me often he liked that I hadn't replaced him. He thought that meant he was irreplaceable. I wanted to let him know that my experience was so bad, I didn't want to risk repeating it.

"I'm actually going. If you can meet me, that would be great. My plane doesn't leave for three hours."

"Baby girl, I'm tired, but I'll think about it. If I don't catch you today, I'll get with you when you get back in town. All right?" He yawned loudly.

I rattled off the airline and other pertinent information and clicked my phone off. I didn't bother telling him that coming back was no certainty.

Besides been drenched, by the time I got settled and situated, I was exhausted. The airport was like a war zone, with a bunch of checkpoints and preventive measures instituted when our country took a major security stand. I waited outside the departure gate, just in case Marco changed his mind, since he was such an unpredictable man.

There was a time when I could read him like a book, but I hadn't been around him for longer than a few hours in much longer than I even wanted to reflect on, and sad to say, those hours weren't spent with either of us saying much. I'm adult enough to call those midnight visits what they were—full-fledged booty calls. But I missed him like crazy, and if having him meant opening my door and allowing him to come in to be with me before climbing in bed later with his flavor of the month, then so be it. What a low point in my life that had been. Actually, that low point started the minute I hopped on that plane with him. I'd never been his audience of one, not even when we were back in Virginia.

I was totally oblivious to what he was really about. He'd moved to Virginia with his aunt after committing some petty crimes in New York. His aunt pleaded with the system, and they slapped him on the wrist, telling her to get him on the next thing smoking out of their city. I won't say he totally lied about the house he and his aunt lived in. It did belong to his grandparents, and after she had the golden opportunity to marry what she considered a good man, she left Marco to take care of himself. She didn't exactly promote his street job, but she didn't discourage it either. How was a sixteen-year-old boy supposed to take care of himself? He did what he had to do and was so good at it and creating his business, he did just that, "took care of his self."

He conducted his evening affairs far away from where we lived, and still he continued to do what he did as if it was in his blood and he just couldn't break away from its grip. Hindsight allowed me to commend him in part, not for what he did—when I found out about it, I was sickened and I knew he was wrong. There was no right in that but, as I said, I commended him because even a dog didn't use the bathroom where they lay their head. There was so much I didn't know then.

Up until this very moment, a part of me still loved Marco. I just couldn't let that love board the plane with me today. It was high time for me to let it go. I desperately needed to free myself from its grip and move on. There's the saying, it's no fool like an old fool, and I had been a fool for twenty-three years.

I busied myself with flipping through an *Ebony* magazine. When I finished that I checked out O, Oprah's monthly magazine. As I read article after article, scanned what was new, and what continued to be hot items, butterflies moved through my stomach. Perhaps it was anticipating Marco's arrival, history maybe I wasn't really sure. All I knew was, I needed to give it all a final rest. Everything. Saying no was never an option, or being real with myself a desire from the time he said hello, to our arrival in Oakland, his deciding he needed space, to the occasional drop-bys to the condo we once shared together, to the quick kiss, after sharing all I was, with the man I loved so much. This man was holding me emotionally like winnings from a high-stakes poker game, and it was time for me to announce that the game was over.

"Hey, baby girl. What's good?" Marco slipped up behind me and stood over me, a confident smile on his face.

I wish I could say that his lifestyle had aged him or changed him for the worst, but Marco looked even better. And when you put designer clothes on a body that was already firm, lean, and well defined, you would expect nothing short of greatness. I knew I didn't look the same, and I worked overtime taking care of myself and my body, hoping that the stress of everything wouldn't get the better of me.

I quickly glanced down at the outfit I'd selected early that morning. Everything was pulled together nicely, from the cuffed gray slacks to sheer black peasant blouse. My Nine West black mules were visible as I sat with my ankles crossed. A visit to my hair salon was a special treat the day before, so every strand of hair was slick and relaxed and hung slightly below the nape of my neck in a stylish bob.

"Hello, Marco." I recognized one of his boys a short distance away. He'd assumed the position of his main bodyguard. He looked at me and nodded his head slightly. I nodded back. I didn't bother to smile at him because he never smiled back. I guess it was to appear hard-core and all about business.

Before I could say a word, Marco closed the distance between us, leaned down and kissed me softly on the lips, lingering there for a second. I blinked a few times to compose myself while he took a seat beside me.

"It's been a while since I've seen or talked to you. You look good though . . . real good." His eyes roamed over me more than once, and after the third or fourth once-over, stopped at my cleavage.

What a difference working out made. I knew I'd never be a size ten, and I would never come close to being considered average-size, but the curves I had were in the right places, and I'd been maintaining them well. It felt good to hear him compliment me, and even better watching his visual appreciation.

"Thanks. You look well." That's all I could say. Anything else would have confirmed what he sat there already knowing. He was many things, and arrogant was among them.

"So tell me, where you going?" Marco leaned back and placed his BlackBerry in his pants pocket.

"I'm going home. Aunt Debbie had a stroke, and Gabby needs my help caring for her."

"Oh, for real? I'm sorry to hear that. That's big of you, leaving your job to help Gabby out. I'm sure she wouldn't bother you unless she needed to," he said, nonchalantly. "Well, I didn't mind getting up out of my comfortable bed, drive across town to this airport, get that nine-one-one and tell you good-bye. That's what significant others do, right?"

The words *significant others* came out of his mouth like he was speaking the truth. And what would he know about one person needing the other? *Need* was foreign to him; it had to be. I'd needed him once, and he walked out.

"Whatever, Marco. But I didn't call you to come down here as my solo bon voyage posse."

"What? You didn't just want to see your sweet daddy? And here I was thinking you wanted me to see you off." He grinned and rubbed his goatee. His hair was freshly cut, and mustache and goatee lined and trimmed. "Do you need money?" He reached down in his pocket and pulled out a wad of bills.

At my lowest financial moment, I had never asked him to front me money, even though the expensive condo was his selection of housing. I didn't feel he was obligated to help pay for a place he didn't want to stay in. I couldn't take anything from him, and worked hard to ensure it stayed that way. Even after becoming a nurse, I took a few private-duty assignments to stay on top and to keep a roof over my head. It would have been easier to let it go and move into something cheaper, but I wanted to prove to him that I could maintain.

I glanced at my purse, reflecting on exactly how much money I had in my account, my one credit card, and the cash from my ATM visit earlier in the week. The total was pitiful, but it was all I had to my name after clearing out some debts and other things that had to be done before I could exit. I was tempted to ask for a few dollars as a backup, a little just-in-case money, but that would make the conversation I was about to have with him meaningless. I'd just make out the best way I could and hope and pray for a financial blessing. Who knows, even though Aunt Debbie couldn't talk, maybe her direct line to glory was still working and God would bless me by association.

"No, Marco, I'm fine." I looked down for a second and then back up at him. My eyes locked with his. It was at this moment that I realized I had been holding on and loving him all this time and he had let me go a long time ago, if in fact he ever held anything more than a desire to conquer all of me, heart, mind, and body. "You know I've loved you for almost a lifetime."

"Shorty, tell me something I don't know." He laughed. "And you've been my baby girl for just as long."

Before he had a chance to add something else meaning-less to what had to be the worst summation of what I was to him, I told him, "You've never been worthy of the love I've given you. I came to Oakland because you said you loved me and wanted me to be your wife. I was young and dumb and bought every word, every story, and every excuse you handed me." I turned away from him, knowing it would be easier to say what needed to be said. "You walked out telling me you needed space, when what you wanted was to reside in anoth-er space with someone else. And even though I knew about Sherri, Kim, and all the others, I allowed you to come back to me in between, whenever you felt the need to remind me that I was nothing but a piece."

"Baby girl, that wasn't the way it was. I can't believe you think so low of me. I was young then." He leaned forward.

"And what is your excuse now, Marco? No, don't even an-swer that. You took my love and all that I had to offer and gave it back to me broken and beyond repair. The few rela-tionships I tried to have ended badly because you took away my ability to trust. Marco, more than that, I waited for the others to do to me what you did, and when they didn't right away, I was so afraid it would happen, I walked away. I don't even know if I could ever love anyone else."

"You act as if loving me has been that bad. We had some good times. You can't sit here and say that it's been all bad."

"Since we've been here, I've been the other woman. I've been in the shadow of so many others, and it's never been just about me and you. How do you think that makes me feel, when I gave up my life to follow you?"

"Cassandra, you blowing this all out of proportion."

"I'm just saying what I should have said when everything about us started going south." I noticed that there was move-ment around the departure gate, which meant I needed to say my good-bye. "Marco, I'm letting you go." I had told myself I wasn't going to cry, but the corner of my eyes began to burn.

"Baby girl, stop talking crazy. Look, your flight is about to board. Go enjoy your family, and we can talk about this when you get back. Here, take this." He flipped through the wad of money he had put back in his pocket.

"Marco, I don't need your money. It's never been about your money, and you know that. What you did and what you are doing was never for me. I never asked you to hustle. I would have loved you if you never had a thing." The tears that threatened started to fall, and I felt so out of control. "It's been twenty-three years, and it's time I end this. I may always love you, but starting today, I'm falling out of love with you. Marco, it's finally over." I picked up my tote bag and purse and stood up. I smiled through the tears and attempted a weak laugh. "It's time that I do me."

Marco stood up and looked down at me. He gave me a blank stare but didn't bother to utter a word. Instead of telling me I had it all wrong and asking me to stay for love's sake, he walked away.

His bodyguard, the same guy who'd never done more than nod in my general direction, walked over to me before catching up with his boss. "Are you okay, Cassandra?"

I had never noticed how handsome he was, perhaps because we never had a face-to-face conversational exchange. His piercing brown eyes seemed so full of concern, concern that I should have seen in Marco's eyes.

I tried to smile. "I'll be fine."

"Here." He reached in his pocket and pulled out a card. "Call me if you need anything or if you just want to talk."

"Doesn't that go against your professional obligation or some kind of boss-employee code?" I reached out to receive the card. Times had truly changed in the game when the kingpin's bodyguard not only carried, but handed out business cards. What in the world was he advertising?

"It is, but something tells me Marco just gave up a good thing."

"You are absolutely right, but I don't have time to cry over the milk he spilled. Thanks for the card." I walked away to the departure gate, where I stood behind a few other passengers.

Glancing over my shoulder, I watched as he walked in the direction Marco had gone. I appreciated his concern. I was hoping he didn't get in trouble for lagging behind when he was hired to be a shadow. Who knew what led him to reach out to me or to give me his business card. He knew I was one of Marco's many women, and since he was his constant companion and had camped out on my living room sofa many nights when Marco decided to spend the night, he was all too aware of the fool I had repeatedly played. I figured Mr. Bodyguard was likely being nice to me, positioning himself to be the rebound guy.

The guy at the gate yelled, "Ms! Ms!"

"Oh, I'm sorry," I said, snapping out of the daydream I had momentarily fallen into. I moved toward him and reached inside the tote for my wallet.

The gentleman looked at my electronic ticket and then inspected my photo ID. "Enjoy your flight. Are you traveling for business or pleasure?"

I thought for a second and responded, "It's pleasure. I'm going home."

Chapter 6

Gabrielle

I was exhausted. Every inch of my body was bone-tired and weary. Even my mind was tired of pushing thoughts, plans, and strategies back and forth. Since Ms. Emma left, I had been living out of two households, mine and my mother's. Two households not only meant going back and forth, but it meant double the chores. There wasn't enough hours in the day for me to do all that I needed to do, so I worked well into the wee hours of the morning just to stay on top of things. Even with two weeks off from the clinic, I was being pulled and stretched beyond normal limits. I spent my days and bedtime hours at Mom's, and in between I'd speed home in time to fix dinner, clean, do laundry, and make sure each of my children and husband had what they needed.

When Mom didn't feel like tagging along, Ma Benson, one of our church mothers, would come over and sit with her while I conducted home business. Maybe I was being my own worst critic. Nothing had fallen apart, and everyone to my knowledge was in one piece mentally and physically.

Even though she couldn't tell me so, Mom was enjoying the extra time I was spending with her. I could see it in her eyes and her slow nods. It was apparent in the slight crooked smile she gave me.

Alexis and Jay were in their own self-absorbed teenage worlds, and unless it was a certain outfit, a particular item that they couldn't find or something that they couldn't make sense of in their thirty-minute or less time limit, they were cool with the partial separation.

Jeffrey, on the other hand, complained daily. None of my balancing act efforts was acceptable or appreciated. There was no doubt he cared about my mother's well-being, but having me step in full-time as her designated caregiver wasn't, in his view, the best solution, even if it was just for a few weeks. Which was why I asked Zee to stay with Mom tonight.

I had told him that Cassie would be in town tomorrow, but he swore he needed to spend an evening with his wife. Zee didn't mind at all. In fact, she had been asking if I needed her to help lighten the load. She even picked up the kids after school and enlisted them to help with their grandma. In return they'd get a trip to the mall to buy something new, dinner, and a movie. I didn't want to bust her bubble, but the kids would have been more than willing to do it for less than her proposed bounty. They were into self, but when it came to their grandma, they did whatever was required.

Zee's latest extension of help was for two reasons. One, she simply wanted to help me out because she loved me and Mom, and two, well, it spoke for itself—Cassie would be coming in town and she didn't want to be outdone. I prayed that she would get over the jealousy she had always harbored toward Cassie, especially after all these years. When Cassie had left all those years ago, Zee became my number one go-to person. I know she was feeling some type of way, knowing that, in a few days and once the awkwardness wore off, Cassie and I would likely be as tight as we always were. At least that is what I prayed. I didn't want to leave Zee out, but I wanted Cassie and I to be the way we were.

Freshly showered, I picked out one of my Vickie pieces. After smoothing some scented body butter over my body and lightly spraying my favorite vanilla-scented body spray, I slipped on a cute little hot pink sheer halter baby doll nightie, complete with matching G-string. I didn't bother to wrap my hair or cover it up with a satin scarf. Instead I twisted it loosely and put a few pins to hold it in place.

I looked in the mirror and was pleased with what I saw. Nothing about me had changed since we got married. Time had been gentle, and I had aged well. Even after two kids, my body was still in great shape. Nothing sagged, and not an inch of me hung lower than it should. Whatever Jeffrey wasn't satisfied with, I didn't want to even think it was the way I looked.

The lights were dim and the ambiance was set. Kenny G flowed from the surround sound speakers, and the tension from the day, and the days before, melted into a longing I couldn't describe. Jeffrey wanted to spend some quality time with me, and although I wasn't thrilled to leave Mom, he was my husband and I needed him just as much.

I was relaxing in the king-size poster bed I shared with my husband, reading a book about rekindling the flame in your marriage. It wasn't that I didn't know what to do in the love-making department, but one should always be willing to make adjustment and improvement here and there, at will and when needed. Actually this was the second time I had read the book. I wanted a refresher, in case I missed something. Jeffrey needed me to give more, do more. He hadn't said it in so many words, but I knew it was what he wanted.

Jeffrey walked out of the bathroom with only a blue towel wrapped around his waist, beads of water glistening on his back and shoulders. "Why are you reading? I thought I'd have your undivided attention." He stopped in front of the dresser mirror and turned his face from side to side, rubbing after-shave moisturizer over his freshly shaven chin and cheeks.

I immediately tossed the book on my nightstand. "I was just reading until you finished taking your shower. I'm all yours."

Jeffrey had been in an awful mood since he walked through the door hours ago. Before I could quiz, he immediately explained that he'd had a bad day at work, and that the next day wouldn't be any better.

We'd made small talk while we ate dinner. Since we had the house to ourselves for the first time in I couldn't remember how long, I went ahead and prepared a special dinner. I grilled steaks, steamed lobster tails, baked potatoes and loaded them with bacon bits, sour cream, feta cheese, and chives. To take care of the vegetable portion of our meal, I tossed a salad and mixed together a house dressing. Jeffrey ate every bite and even polished off the remainder of bread pudding left over from the night before.

I was going to do something about his mood in about ten minutes or less, but right now I was fixated on his body. He worked out religiously, and his body was so well toned, his muscles tensed and rippled with almost every move he made.

"It's about time." Jeffrey mumbled a few others words before turning off the light.

I held my breath as he dropped the towel and slipped in bed beside me. After he settled under the sheet and adjusted his pillows, I waited for him to reach out to me. What I desired was for him to caress and kiss me lightly. My body wanted—actually, wanted was putting it mildly—it *needed* to be awakened by the feel of him against my skin. The thought of his passionate lovemaking made me instantly weak. He always knew how to please me, and although we hadn't done it like that in a while, I knew he was more than capable of tripping all of my lights from red to green. I wasn't sure why I was mentally feeling Jeffrey like this, but I closed my eyes and went with it.

After another minute, I decided to reach out to him. He did say he had a rough day, so I wasn't going to be selfish. I began to rub his chest, and he moaned a little. "Turn over," I whispered softly.

When he did, I reached in the drawer of my nightstand and took out some shea butter and coconut massage oil. I blew on the liquid, and it warmed against the palm of my hand. Smiling, I straddled him and began to massage his back and shoulders.

He began to speak real deep, "Oh, yes! That feels so good. That's what I'm talking 'bout. Oh, yes!"

The more I rubbed and squeezed, the more he told me how good it felt. I wasn't a sex-starved kitten or anything close, but this was my husband, and I had a right to enjoy every minute of whatever we did in the privacy of our bedroom. And right now I was enjoying him telling me how good I was making him feel. Focusing was becoming harder and harder, and heck I missed him, so I was already on my way to our end zone, following the make-me-holla course.

Even before Ms. Emma had to leave, our physical love interactions had been limited, and when we did make a connection, it was rushed and hurried. Tonight seemed so promising, and I didn't want to miss the boat or waste another moment.

I leaned down and kissed his neck and nibbled at his right ear and then his left.

Jeffrey moaned even more. "I need you." He lifted his head off the pillow slightly, his breathing heavy and full of a familiar lust.

That was exactly what I wanted to hear. I moved so he could turn over completely. Falling slowly against my oversized pillow, I closed my eyes again and mentally relaxed into another past memory of us. It sent a chill down my spine, and I smiled in the darkness. "I love you."

He mumbled something back that wasn't even audible, and while it didn't sound all that romantic, I didn't dwell. Jeffrey moved on top of me. There was no kiss, no caress, and no fingertip touches against my flesh. In the space where our passion should have ignited with mini-fireworks, my husband gave me what he thought I needed and what he had been waiting for.

I tried to slow him down a few times, to somehow send a physical message that I wanted this to last, wanted our coming together to be more than this. My caresses and touches received no response, and before I could even join in, Jeffrey exhaled loudly, trembled a couple of times, and then ceased all movement. Without one word or anything else that could have been viewed as a romantic gesture, he collapsed on his side of the bed.

"What's wrong?" I was almost afraid to ask. The last thing I needed was for him to think I was complaining about his lovemaking skills. It wasn't about the skills, it was more about what was going on that made everything about us out of sync, with no connection.

"Nothing's wrong. That's what happens when you stay away forever, Gabrielle. You expect me to be a Duracell bunny after you've been in and out of here for the past two weeks, all the while I'm on hold. Besides, it don't take all night."

I curled up behind him.

"Gabby, I'm tired."

"Oh, okay." I moved away feeling hurt, disappointed and not understanding the why and the what. This wasn't totally new. It'd happened many times before, and each time I ended up empty in more ways than one. Wasn't he the same person who was saying I needed to come home to be with him? Obviously, the plan of pleasure didn't include me.

The morning went by in a blur as I busied myself with cooking breakfast, bacon, eggs, home fries, and blueberry muffins. I hummed despite my short-lived night of passion. In spite of how it all ended, I was in a good mood. I'd opened my eyes to a bright sunny morning, and before my feet hit the floor, leaned over and kissed Jeffrey on the cheek. Someone bigger than me was navigating my course today, because I just knew I would be depressed and upset, and here I was bubbling over with good feelings.

"Hey. How'd you make out last night?" I looked over the island as I spoke to Zee on the house phone and placed the hot muffins in a basket. Tilting my head, I looked in the direction of the stairs to see if Jeffrey was coming down.

"Just fine. Ma Debbie was a dear, and the kids entertained her with story after story until almost nine o'clock. By the time we got her in bed and situated, she was out like a light."

"That's good. I know she enjoyed your company too. Mom was probably bored with me, and if she could, she'd likely tell me just that."

"I doubt it. Ma Debbie thinks you are the sun, the stars, and the moon." Zee laughed.

She was telling the truth. Mom would point out character flaws, but then she'd list a dozen other attributes that she was so proud of.

"I know. Are the kids up and moving?"

"Yep. The smell of sausage had them moving. They're waiting for me to finish up everything. It took a while to get in here because I wanted to get Ma Debbie bathed and situated. She's really good at doing a lot for herself though."

"I know. She is so independent, despite everything. Listen, are you still okay with staying with her while I pick Cassie up from the airport?"

"Oh, her. Is today the day she comes in?" Zee's words trailed off in sarcasm.

"Yes, and you know it." I glanced up just as Jeffrey walked in the kitchen dressed in sweatpants and a T-shirt."

"We will be fine. The kids are going to hang around, and who knows what we may get into. Don't sweat what's going on over here. Just go get what's her name. We don't want to risk her getting back on a plane and returning to the black hole she climbed out of—I mean, where she came from."

"You are being bad, but thanks for helping out. I'll tell Cassie you can't wait to see her." I giggled as I watched Jeffrey return back in from getting the paper. I was trying to gauge where he was emotionally, but I couldn't tell. He pulled out a chair from the kitchen table, waiting for me to get his food.

"Whatever. I'm out." Zee hung up.

I knew she was just as anxious to see Cassie as I was. At least, I was hoping.

Mom had smiled when I mentioned that Cassie was coming to help take care of her. From the time she had left, the void was obvious. She'd call her name by mistake or talk about something Cassie would do or say. And after Dad died she missed her even more. Mom would walk out on the back porch many evenings and just stare at the driveway. She never said a word, but I knew she expected Cassie to show up. I smiled to myself because my mother's wish would be coming true.

"Good morning." I placed the phone back in the cradle and began to fix Jeffrey's plate.

"Dag! I thought you were going to talk all morning." He flipped through the paper and didn't bother to look up at me. "The food is probably cold."

"It can't be. I just took the muffins out of the oven, and the food is in the warmer." I poured coffee in his mug and added a little sugar and hazelnut creamer. Then I put the food on his plate and placed it in front of him. I wanted to say something about his remark but decided against it.

"What time are you leaving to pick up Cassie?" He put the paper to the side, blessed his food, and began to eat.

"Not for another hour. Her plane lands at three. Since I won't have time to fix dinner, I thought I would order everything from The Rib Joint and pick it up on the way in."

"If that's what you want to do."

I was across from him, and yet he talked to me with his head down. The food was tasty, I was sure, but I would've appreciated being able to look into his eyes.

"I just thought it would be nice. We can have everything at Mom's. That way Zee won't have to pack Mom up and bring her here." I pushed my food around on my plate. I was suddenly full. The good feeling was slipping away.

"Well, I'll try to be there on time," he said with no real emotion. He was saying he wasn't sure, but it didn't sound as if he cared one way or the other. This would be his first time meeting Cassie.

I was excited, but I guess not everyone shared that excitement. "What would prevent you from being there when I return?" I stood up and removed our plates from the table.

"For one, I'm going to work out with Todd and Nate and then we plan on running ball for a few hours. After that who knows. There's a game on and you know they have high stakes in who they think will win. I don't get into that, but I always like telling them how wrong they are." He chuckled, as if I should find some amazement in his friends recreational betting.

"Well, why don't you invite them over, and they can have dinner with us. And you guys can watch the game on the big-screen we bought Mom for Christmas. The only time she lets anyone turn it on is when we are all together watching a movie or a DVD from a church service." I held my breath, hoping that inviting his friends would be enough to encourage him to be there for a family gathering.

"That might work. I'll see what they think." He came up behind me and wrapped his arms around my waist.

I relaxed a little and felt something stirring on the inside, but I didn't say a word. I really didn't know what to say or how to respond to his up-and-down yo-yo move.

"I know I've been difficult, but as I said, I got a lot going on, and there's a lot of pressure at work. You deciding to stay at your Mom's, despite my input, hasn't really helped at all."

"She's my mom, Jeffrey. She doesn't need someone she doesn't know moving in with her. Besides, Cassie is coming, and it would have just been too much and too many gears to shift."

"I know, but my way would have been the better way. With someone trained and understanding that its their job, you wouldn't have to rely on Ms. Emma or call Cassie to come across country. Even better, there are assisted living facilities."

"Stop. I will not ever consider that. Mom is vibrant and still in good shape. It was a stroke. It didn't take away all of her faculties."

"See, that's the problem. You won't look at it the way it is. Always seeing with closed eyes." He moved away from me.

"That's not true. I just don't think we're at that stage of the game."

Both of my husband's parents had passed. His father died before we got married, and his mother a few years after we got married. I couldn't understand why he wanted me to put my mother in a facility. He had stood by his mother's side until the end, and even when her health declined and the Alzheimer's set in, he refused to move her out of their family home. He said something about wanting her in a familiar setting. On top of that, he had no trouble having me stay over many nights to care for her while he was at home. He would tell me that his mom had needs that needed a female's attention. I never said a word because I saw it as my obligation. He was my husband, so she was as much my mother as his when I stood before God and said, "I do."

"Well, I just might bring the boys over so they can get a look at your cousin. From the photos I've seen, she was a beautiful girl." He walked back over and leaned against the counter. "They will likely want first crack at her. New eye candy, if nothing else."

"That is so wrong."

He was right. Cassie was beautiful. The first time Jeffrey saw a photo of us, he remarked about how much we looked alike, being the daughters of sisters. He wasn't the first person to make that observation. We knew it too, and it made our bond all the more special.

"It's the truth. Why wait and let some other hounds get a bark? I look out for my boys. I want them to know what it's like to have a beautiful woman on their arm."

"I didn't know you noticed." I felt a surge of reassurance.

"I don't miss anything. Of course, I don't have to comment now or do all that overboard stuff. You should know how I feel. It all goes without saying. I'm out. Hit me when you get across the bridge. Listen, if it will make things easier, I'll pick up the food from The Rib Joint."

"You know Zee will be there, right?" I put my hand on my hip and threw the towel over my shoulder. I didn't want him to pop in, see Zee, and pop out. I decided to go a step further. "Maybe, you can hook her up—"

"Girl, I'm not a miracle worker."

"And what you really want to say is that Zee is a little bigger than me and a little harder to sell, right?"

"You got it. I know big girls need love too, but I just don't have friends that prefer it that way." He threw both hands up. "Now, I could see past the weight, because she really isn't that big, but as I've told her countless times, she got a bad attitude. You may want to counsel her on that."

"Whatever, Jeffrey. There isn't anything wrong with Zee. I'm going to laugh real hard if you get your boys to come over and Cassie has put on like fifty pounds."

"Don't joke like that." He looked serious. "Is that possible?

I mean, none of the women I've met in your family are heavy-set."

I started walking away laughing. It wasn't that I believed that Cassie had put on weight. I mean, it was possible, because anything was possible. I just didn't like men that had a problem with larger sisters. Zee was a beautiful girl and had so much going for her, and many times she was overlooked just because she wasn't top-model thin. Yeah, I knew she was a little rough where men were concerned, but that was because she had been played by a few brothers who'd proclaimed they were in it for the long haul, only to bounce the minute she didn't finance their future, or cater to them like they were kings. Zee definitely didn't deal with the drama they were dishing out, and if her being direct and blunt rendered her manless, then I'd have to agree with my friend. It was truly their loss. She had better things to do with her time than to deal with brothers who weren't worth the time of day.

"I'm going to get dressed. Time is ticking, and I don't want to be late picking Cassie up."

"Gabby, that ain't even funny. What should I tell my boys?"

Continuing toward the bedroom, I replied, "Tell them she could be a brickhouse or she could be pleasingly plump. Either way, she got it going on. Later, sweetie." I turned around and blew him a kiss. "I'll see you and your boys later."

It felt so good to laugh and joke with Jeffrey. Our conversations and times together hadn't been this light in a while. Of course, I hadn't forgotten what had happened last night. How could I? But I wanted to be hopeful and believe that this could be the beginning of a change for us. There was no way I was going to be consumed with how long it was going to last, allowing doubt to overshadow what felt good right now.

I decided to dwell on being hopeful as I walked up the steps toward our bedroom with a new stride. My intention for today was just to enjoy it. "He thinks I'm still beautiful," I said out loud. "My man thinks I still got it going on." *What a relief!*

SPRING

"The storm will pass. The spring will come."
—Robert H. Schuller

Chapter 7

Cassandra

Even sandwiched between an older gentleman, a young woman with two screaming kids hanging onto her skirt tail, and circles of people closing in, I couldn't miss Gabrielle as she fought with both elbows in mid-air, trying to find space to get a good view of the schedule prompter. Before I saved her the agony of being swallowed in the crowd, letting her know that my plane had landed and I was here, safe and sound, I wanted a chance to just take in the sight of her. Without moving or even blinking, I gazed at her from a short distance for a minute or two.

The moment was here, and now that it was, I wasn't sure what I should say or do. I hadn't seen Gabrielle in forever, and yet looking at her even from where I was standing caused something melancholy to stir on the inside of my being. A part of me felt like it was just yesterday, and not all these years ago. The other part reinforced that a look in the mirror would erase that thought. Yet in my heart and soul, we were right back in the thick of that time.

I'd pleaded with myself before I boarded the plane, during the entire flight and even after it eased to a complete stop and allowed its passengers to exit, to keep up a barrier and not get caught up in an emotional web that would impede my return to California or anywhere that would be my starting-over locale. All I wanted was to care for Aunt Debbie, which I hoped would be short-term, and a simple, unconnected task.

It wasn't my intention to arrive for duty totally heartless, but I couldn't exactly walk in and display my innermost feelings for all of them to see. True to what I had shared with Gabby on the phone, I wanted to give something back for all that my aunt had given me when I was much too young to appreciate and honor the family love she extended like an olive branch. While I never got the nerve to break the silence on my own, this would give me the opportunity to correct the wrong of walking out without her blessing. There was only one mandate I charged myself with, to leave my heart at the door.

But here stood the one person who was like my second skin, and I felt so wrong for cutting her out of my life. Gabby deserved better from me, and now that I was standing here, I knew I had to fix it, to somehow fix us. I didn't want to leave again and not have her connected by more than letters, cards, and holiday photos.

I pushed through the crowd until I was close enough for her to hear me. "I see you've turned over a new leaf. The Gabby I knew would have been here an hour or two ahead of time. What a difference time makes."

Gabby spun around so fast, she almost lost her balance and nearly tipped the elderly gentleman over. She reached out toward him in an apologetic gesture and immediately turned toward me, her mouth opened wide. It took a second for words to come out. "Cassie! Oh my God! Look at you!"

Just as I thought they would, tears began to fall uncontrollably. She was just as beautiful as she was the day I'd walked away from our house. Her eyes, though, looked as if they had witnessed so much and had taken the weight of it all until it filled her soul. Much of it likely didn't make sense, and she always needed things to make sense. The always-alert look and stare was more solemn. Yet I knew somewhere beyond what I could see had to be the person who thrived on life and living, holding on, believing and trusting that a silver lining would come.

"Look at you," I said.

By the time she unraveled herself from the throng of people, I wrapped my arms around her, and we both cried tears of joy. We released each other for a second, only to embrace again. People passing us were smiling, marveling in two people who had obviously been separated for far too long.

"Come on. We'd better get out of here before someone reports two women standing at the baggage claim losing it emotionally." Gabby laughed.

I joined in with her, and the heaviness and hesitation about this moment with my best friend cousin lifted and in its place was the ease that already felt familiar. I placed my knockoff designer tote over my shoulder and turned to retrieve the handles of the two matching wheeled Pullman suitcases. I extended one toward Gabby. "Do you mind helping me out?"

"Of course not," she said, beaming in my direction.

My luggage was stylish, and although I couldn't afford the real thing, I wanted to at least look like I had it going on. If I was lucky, no one would get close enough to see I was perpetrating a fashion fraud. I doubted very seriously whether our small hometown was equipped with fashion police on every corner like Oakland. Then again, I wasn't sure what was on every other corner.

"Did you come by yourself?"

Gabby pulled the handle out from the other suitcase, and we both fell in step together. "Yes. Alexis and Jay are with Mom. Wait until you meet them. Alexis has so much attitude, and Jay thinks he's a little mack." She stopped suddenly.

"Go ahead. Continue. I may not have kept in touch like

I should have, but I read every single letter, and I kept every photo." I felt so awful.

With the exclusion of Aunt Debbie, the people she talked about were strangers to me. Beyond the very basics, I had no clue about Gabby's family, my family. I had certainly made a mess of all of this. It was clear I would have to clean up and do major damage control. I was trying to erase so much, and in the process, I eliminated what mattered more than I knew.

We had walked the long distance from the airport baggage claim area to the parking lot. Gabby moved to the back of a Ford Explorer and opened the cargo area. "Listen, let me say this before we go any further."

We both put the luggage in the back, and just as she closed everything up, she continued, "I'm not sure what was on your mind when you left. I can only imagine. And, yes, for a long time I was hurt, confused, and didn't understand how you could leave me. Everybody else, maybe, but not me. Cassie, I was so mad at you. But that was then, and this is now. I've come to realize that you must have had your reasons. You just chose not to share those reasons with me."

"I wish it had been that easy." There was no way I could tell her that it wasn't just about riding off into the sunset with Marco.

"For what it's worth, I'm not mad anymore. I have-n't been for a while. My only prayer is that whatever needed to heal was healed, and you are returning whole."

"Thank you for that." I touched her arm, reached for her hand, and locked my fingers with hers. "I never meant to hurt you."

I couldn't tell her everything, but I could tell her that Marco never married me, despite the lies I wrote them. I could even add that many of the days since I left had been rough. Or I could skip all that, fast-forward to a month ago, and give her the quick and abbreviated version—that my job downsized, and right before she contacted me, I was on the verge of not knowing what to do. All or any of that would have made me the hopeless misfit I always felt I was. No, I couldn't tell her, even though she was my rock. She deserved more from me, more from my life.

In so many ways, that was why I didn't keep in touch. Other than pushing my way through school and working day and night just to survive, what had my life come to? Very little. Gabby was the mother of two wonderful, bright kids, and the apple of her husband's eye. She had graduated from college and even went on to get a master's degree. I was sure everyone was proud and expected nothing less from her, all of this accomplished under the watchful eye of my aunt. All the more reason everything I said from this point on would be exaggerated and spun with enough crafty add-ons to sound so believable, no one would dare question me.

I cleared my throat. "I got so caught up in the good life that, before I knew it, so much time had passed. I did think of you often."

Gabby looked back at me as if shocked that I was speaking of good life and losing time, and she on the other hand had just granted me a pardon by forgiving me for being cold and breaking her heart with my abrupt departure. I knew she expected me to say more than that after all this time, but I couldn't.

I decided just then, it would be best to cleverly cover my tracks. There was no way she or anyone else could have known anything about my life there.

She blinked back the emotion and smiled really hard. "I understand. What matters is that we needed you, and thank God you are here."

"I sure am. Now, let's get going." I needed to lighten the zone we had entered. "The kids probably need a break. Babysitting is probably not one of their top ten things to do on a

Saturday." I didn't have any kids of my own, but I could only imagine an array of activities that would have been preferred.

"Zee is with them." Gabby clicked her keyless entry button, and we both climbed in. She fastened her seat belt, pulled the visor down, and put on her sunglasses. She repeated, "Zee is with them," looking in my direction before starting the car.

"Heard you the first time. Zee is still around, huh?"

There was no love lost between me and Zenith, who spent all of her time trying to sway Gabby her way, to prove she was the better friend. I could never say I didn't see it. I did from day one, way back when we were playing on the monkey bars, the swings, and the seesaws.

It was just Gabby who was slow to recognize Zee's manipulative ways. Even when she began to see it, she wanted to believe that Zee meant no harm and just wanted to make our twosome a threesome. In short, a little of Zee went a long way with me. It was going to be interesting to see if age and wisdom would make our chilly relationship any warmer.

"She's all grown up, just like us. So much has changed with her. You'll see it for yourself." Gabby sounded so confident.

"I see." That was the only safe thing I could say. "She probably thought I was taking *witch* airline instead of Southwest."

Gabby chuckled. "I can't believe you remember Zee calling you a witch whenever things got tense between you two."

"How could I forget that? It happened like every other day."

I joined in Gabby's amusement. Those were some hilarious days. I was a true troublemaker at heart and would start stuff just to get Zee on the rampage. Our shouting matches and arguments never turned into fights, but there were days when we were two seconds from a throw-down.

"Seriously, though, I know she had a few things to say

about my visit home." I tilted my head and looked directly at Gabby, as if warning her to tell the whole truth.

"She didn't say anything negative."

The exit leaving the airport was congested with traffic. Gabby slowed down and braked as others maneuvered around us.

"You know you never could lie—Excuse me, let me rephrase that—elude the truth."

"Thank you for rephrasing that. You know Mom would have a fit if she thought either of us was telling an out-and-out lie."

We both laughed. We must have shared the same visual of Aunt Debbie holding her hands up to the heavens asking for forgiveness for her children.

"You are right about that." I reached for my purse that was placed on the floor and pulled out my cell phone from the side pocket. "Looks like I have a message."

I dialed voice mail and put the phone against my ear to listen. The voice was immediately recognizable. He asked if my plane had landed and ended by reminding me that I should use the card if I needed anything. I immediately dismissed the call. He was probably calling for Marco, and any information I shared with him would be information that he likely was paid to get. I blocked the number from coming through and then erased it. Not that it mattered, because by tomorrow or later today, he could have a new cell phone or new cell number. I wanted nothing to do with Marco or anyone connected to him ever again, no matter how nice his front man was. There had to be something in it for him. It was high time and long overdue, but everything about Marco and I was over.

Gabby looked over. "You okay?"

We maneuvered to the interstate, and Gabby was cruising along carefully, methodically, and according to the speedometer, well within the speed limit. Cars, SUVs, and big rig trucks swiftly breezed past us on the way to their destination, with no respect for drivers like Cassie, concerned about getting to their destination safely.

"Everything is fine. Just a check-in-call."

I leaned back against the leather of the seat. I knew we had at least a two-hour drive, so I decided to just relax and window-watch. Though sleep had eluded me for the past few nights, I was too hype, too curious to close my eyes. I didn't want to miss a thing. There were likely some major chain stores, or strip malls added or houses and developments on land that used to grow some of the Eastern Shore's famous crop. I didn't expect skyscrapers or the like, but I was sure whatever was along the route would be a real eye-opener. I'd have to wait until later to catch up on some rest. Spending my days in the house with Aunt Debbie would surely give me a lot of time to rest.

"Don't tell me Marco misses you already."

"I guess you can say that. He reminded me to call if I needed anything."

I was hoping my voice didn't seem unusual for a woman who was living the "happily ever after." I didn't want to keep lying to her, and I knew sooner or later, she along with everyone else would start asking more questions about Marco. I figured it was best if I stayed a few steps ahead and provide information before they could go through twenty-one questions of the how, what, when. No, I would have to decide what or how I would disclose the facts or the exaggerated facts of my marriage to my teenage sweetheart. What a web I was weaving. I didn't want to exit stage left and leave Gabby with more questions than answers yet again, but this task needed to be over soon so I could live a life free of demons. I needed new.

Gabby smiled. "Oh, okay."

She began to talk about Aunt Debbie, giving me the latest medical updates and what they believed had led to the stroke. She was always a vibrant go-getter and that hadn't changed.

In fact, after Uncle Ed died, according to Gabby, she became even busier. They believed it was to get over the loss, but she reached a point where it was all so overwhelming and her physical body couldn't take all that it had shouldered for decades. Not to mention how taxing and draining it was to care for a flock of church sheep whose needs were always put before her own. I guess when it was put this way and all things considered, Aunt Debbie's stroke was an accident waiting to happen, and family medical history made her an heir to vascular and circulatory mishaps.

I listened and remarked, adding my theory and experiences with stroke patients. At least what I was sharing was real, and in many ways, I believed I could help Aunt Debbie.

"Oh, listen to this." I leaned forward and turned the radio up.

Gabby glanced at the radio as if looking to see who it was, instead of just listening. "Isn't that Midnight Star?"

"Yes, girl. It's 'Slow Jam.' Gosh! Do you remember us dancing with Rick and Tony at the homecoming dance? We were dancing side by side, and both of us thought we were in love." I giggled, remembering how, in the wee hours of the morning, we'd talk about what it would be like to marry them.

"How could I forget that."

"My, my, my." I smiled.

We both were silent, as if reflecting for a moment, and then we started singing along with the song. I bounced my head and snapped my fingers, and Gabby was right with me. The station continued to play oldies but goodies, and we sang and recapped along the way.

By the time we hit the bridge, I was completely mellow and felt so light and free of all of my cares. I gazed out over the water and watched it as it rippled and moved back and forth. The sky above was so picture-perfect and seemed to merge into the water's edge. My eyes were fixated, and the soothing effects pulled me gently. Never before had I seen anything as beautiful. If I did, I guess the beauty of it escaped me because life had not slowed down enough for me to truly embrace it, and all its bright possibilities.

The last time I'd crossed this bridge I was with Marco. I guess I was so focused on my new life with him that the ocean was the last thing on my mind. On my finger was the "promise ring" he had given me the minute I got in the car. I was so hyped with the reality that it was the beginning and very soon he would be my husband and I'd be his wife. Mrs. Cassandra Brent. I didn't even want to keep Price in my name at all. Forget the hyphenated thing, all I needed to be was Mrs. Brent. Crazy, young, and foolishly in love is what I was. Years later the youth disappeared, but the crazy and foolishly in love stayed around.

Gabby's phone interrupted my thoughts.

She clicked her earpiece. "Hello," she said. "Well, I'm about forty-five minutes away, so go ahead and get everything together. Why can't you?" she asked, raising her voice a little.

When she turned toward me, I turned to look out the window.

"The plan was set, and I'd appreciate it if you follow through. Please." She clicked off the phone.

"Is everything okay?"

"Oh, yeah. Our timing was just sort of off. It's all good." Gabby rubbed the back of her neck with her right hand and twisted in her seat a little.

"That looks like tension."

I could tell that Gabby was dealing with some stuff that was wearing her down. It was on her face when I first saw her again, and now her body was displaying all the signs. It may have just been Aunt Debbie, and crowding all of those needs in with the needs of her family. Then, of course, there was her job. Listening to other people's problems day in day out and having to patiently give them a healthy view free of bias and old-fashioned wit or just plain good sense. I was sure she thought about telling some of her patients to just get a spine or jump, but that wouldn't be good for business.

"Yeah. Every evening around this time, it starts. It's no big deal." She pushed past her health and began to talk about some renovations she wanted to make to the family house.

As we went back and forth, my eyes were taking in everything along the way. So much had changed. If I didn't know this was the right way to get to where we were going, I wouldn't have known, since there were no familiar landmarks or anything on the main route that I remembered.

Before I knew it, we turned on Lark Street. I closed my eyes for a second. As soon as we turned, it was a contrast to the last hour. Everything on our street was almost exactly as it was years ago. It was as if this area was untouched by time. My stomach cringed, and I felt as if I had suddenly stepped straight into the clutches of menopause. I started fanning myself with a envelope that was on the dashboard.

Gabby noticed my sudden reaction. "It's going to be okay, you'll see."

I couldn't speak. I could only smile slightly. Much too quickly, Gabby was signaling a right turn. In the short distance stood the two-story Victorian-style house that was my home long ago. It wasn't beige anymore. It was now white and had brown and beige marble brick midway down. The steps were wider and were made of the same type brick, and off to the side was a handicap ramp. The rest of the yard was as neat as I remembered it, with rose and azalea plants and lush green bushes all around.

Juat as Gabby turned off the car and turned to me, the front door opened, and a teenage girl, who looked much like the two of us in our youth, and a handsome young man came running out of the house with wide smiles on their faces.

Zee maneuvered the wheelchair with Aunt Debbie to the wide steps, and they stood there watching as we got out of the car.

"Cassie, we're home."

"Yes," I said, "home."

Chapter 8

Gabrielle

Alexis came storming into the kitchen as Zee and I were putting the dishes away. "Mom, Aunt Cassie is way cool."

Once Jeffrey arrived with his friends in tow, it didn't take long for the food to be set out, and the dinner bell rang to announce it was time to break bread and enjoy a soul food moment. It seemed that, in no time at all, everything had fallen in place.

Cassie seated herself beside Mom's wheelchair, and somehow, between holding hands and just looking at one another, they managed to eat a little. No one else penetrated or invaded their private moment.

"She is pretty cool, isn't she?" I giggled. This was the first time I heard Alexis refer to anyone my age as way cool. The usual adjectives were *old*, *whack*, and *ancient*. She must not have known that there were many grown people, me included, that had the capability of bringing cool back and who, back in the day, were considered the coolest among their respective groups.

As I reflected, it actually wasn't that long ago. Somehow though, Cassie had managed to hold on to a youthful attitude. Maybe it was because of her bedside manner and the reality that many of her older patients likely had the mentality of a child and she constantly had to switch gears to meet them on their level.

Jay was hanging on to every word Cassie uttered, smiling every time she directed her attention toward him.

"Why don't you and Auntie Zee act like that?" Alexis leaned over my shoulder and grabbed a wing off the tray that I was about to wrap.

"Probably because we grew up and we have real lives with real issues and real responsibilities," Zee told her.

I cut my eye at Zee before responding for the both of us. "Well, sweetie, it's just that no two people act the same way. Cassie has always been a free spirit. That's not to say that I can't cut loose, 'cause I can." I playfully hit her butt and did a crazy pose for her.

"Whatever Mom. *Cool* and *corny* are not the same thing." She rolled her eyes. "I'm going to ask Dad if he recalls you ever being a free spirit. I know it's a total waste of time, but what the *hey*." She walked out of the kitchen and in the direction of the family room where Jeffrey, Jay, Todd, and Nate were.

"I could have concluded the answer on my behalf." Zee placed the towel over her shoulder and walked over to me. "Your answer was very colored."

"I know, but I don't think Alexis was asking you. In fact, you know what, Zee? You have been the opposite of what I expected tonight. I know we talked about Cassie, and I really thought I had gotten my point across."

"And what exactly was your point? Do you mind telling me again?" Zee's voice was full of sarcasm.

I inhaled and tried to count to five before I answered, but I only made it to three before I let it rip. "The point was that I wanted—no, scratch that—needed you two to get along. Jesus Christ! You'd think I asked you to give the girl a kidney."

Ever since Cassie had walked in the house, Zee went out of her way to comment negatively on everything that she said, and when Cassie shared a point, she was quick to cross-examine, like Cassie was on the witness stand in a court of law. She didn't grand stand or come totally out of the box on her, but it was noticeable by me, if by no one else. Not even Jeffrey had said anything or acted as if he was slightly offended or concerned by what Zee said or how she may have responded, and God knows he would have been the first person to put Zee in her place, whether Mom was there or not. I was a little sensitive to the situation. I knew I just wasn't going to let this beginning be our ending, or our middle for that matter.

"Wait a minute. I guess Cassie's actions went unnoticed."

"What actions, Zee? Everything within my listening that Cassie said or asked you was above board." I inhaled and exhaled. I needed to reel myself in.

The evening had gone too well for me to let this mess it all up. Jeffrey had even arrived on time, got everything we needed and more. He came in the house and acted the way a husband should act. He even fussed over me a few times and embraced me at all the right times. Of course, it crossed my mind that it could have been all a show for Cassie eyes, but it didn't stop me from enjoying the attention. I'd worry about the public display later, if need be.

Mom managed a smile every time she watched me and my husband interact. I hadn't said a word to her about the bumps we'd been experiencing. I suppose mother wit stepped in, because she acted as if she was relieved that we were more than civil, and it all seemed like old times.

"And what was that about? Nate and Todd don't even know Cassie, and they were falling all over her. They were about ready to fight over who was going to pour tea in her glass. Then I thought Todd was going to do the deed of drinking it for her. I was about ready to throw up."

Zee threw herself in one of the side chairs at the kitchen table and picked up a rib that was covered with barbecue sauce. She bit into the meat and licked her lips, wiping the sauce that dripped down her chin with the back of her hand. She had turned down every offering of meat the entire evening, telling everyone she was on a strict diet and had decided not to partake of any red meat for a month or so. This must had been a "rush" diet, because I didn't know anything about it when she finished off the pork chops I'd cooked Mom a few days before.

"I thought it was cute." I didn't bother to turn around. I knew my response pissed her off.

Cassie came in with a wide smile on her face. She had changed into gray sweats, a plain white tank top, and pink slippers. Seeing her in lounging attire sort of made it official that she was going to be here a while.

"Hey. What you girls talking about without the third musketeer?"

"Nothing much. Just chitchatting while cleaning up," I said over my shoulder. "I see you've changed into your relax gear."

"Yeah. I needed to put on something I could actually take a deep breath in. Those ribs and chicken hit me right around the middle, but, God, were they good." She rubbed her stomach and looked toward Zee, who was finishing up the rib.

Zee could have commented. I could see it all over her face, but she smiled instead.

"I can help you guys out. I was just talking to Aunt Debbie. She hasn't changed at all." Cassie went about the room covering up dishes and wiping things down.

"Did you manage to notice that Ma Debbie is in a wheelchair and can't talk?"

I turned around, but before I could respond, Cassie put her hand up. "No, Gabby. I got this." She walked over to where Zee was sitting and put down the towel she was holding. "Listen, I haven't missed any of your underhanded and borderline-nasty remarks that you have made toward me all night. I chose not to respond because, frankly, I just walked in the door, and this is the first family gathering we have had in years."

"And whose fault is that?" Zee lifted her left hand up and examined her nails before flicking her tongue across her teeth.

"I know whose fault it is, and I'm woman enough to admit my poor judgment call where my family is concerned. But you are not the judge and jury on this case, and let me inform you now that I will not tolerate you disrespecting me or talking out of your neck toward me. If you continue, trust me, Zee, you will seriously catch a case, and it won't be pretty." Cassie started to turn around but stopped. "And another thing . . . don't make me your dumping pad. If your life wasn't star-studded before I got here, and those two out there—What are their names?—Nate and Todd weren't knocking down your door, sweetie, that's not my problem. If it's counseling you need for your issues, I'm sure Gabby can create a slot for you in her very busy, very demanding schedule. There should be some kind of employee discount you can get."

Zee couldn't say a thing. Cassie had cut her to the core. I wish I could say she didn't deserve it. She looked as if she wanted me to tell Cassie to ease up or back off, but I wasn't going to do that, not after she had decided to be a one-woman army against my cousin.

"Cassie, could you see if Mom wants anything else before I put the food in the refrigerator."

"No problem, Gabby." Cassie made her way into the living room with a little more twist than was necessary, glancing over her shoulder to make sure Zee didn't miss her departure.

Just then, there was a knock at the backdoor. I was the closest, so I pulled the curtain back and then reached to unlock and open the door.

"Hey, Blaine. How are you?" I reached my hand out to shake his hand but was greeted with a smile and a warm hug.

"Hello there, Gabby. How's it going?" He walked farther

into the kitchen, so I could close the door behind him. "I hope you don't mind me dropping by, but Jeffrey called and invited me to watch the game with them." He looked at his watch. "I know it's almost over, but I was making a few rounds at the hospital and thought I'd at least catch the ending."

"Don't tell me you are a part of the b-ball game madness?" I put my hand on my hip and pointed a finger at him.

"Guilty as charged." He held both hands up and gave me a Colgate smile. "I don't consider myself an overboard sports fanatic, but I must say, I'm an avid basketball and football fan." He laughed, the sound of his laughter so rich.

"Oh, hello, Blaine. I was on my way in to catch the rest of the game myself." Zee had gotten up from the table and was standing directly beside me.

I looked at her, totally confused. She was just going back and forth with me over Cassie, and at no point did she say anything about watching the game or joining Jeffrey and the boys. Heaven forbid, if she even for a moment sat down beside Jeffrey and expressed interest in something that he knew she had no knowledge of.

"I didn't know you were a basketball watcher?" Blaine raised an eyebrow in her direction.

Probably because he had never seen her at any of the church team games, but I wasn't going to nudge her and bring that tidbit to light.

"Doesn't everyone?" She threw her head back and ran her fingers through her twists.

"No, not everyone." Cassie came in the room and leaned against the kitchen island. She knew Zee was never into sports and she probably would guess that, while she'd picked up a lot of things after her departure, sports watching or playing wasn't one of them.

Zee threw her a look that could cut glass. "Cassie, you know I love the game." She pulled her eyes away from Cassie and looked back at Blaine.

"And who is this?" Blaine asked.

"Oh, Blaine, this is my cousin Cassandra, but we all call her Cassie." I smiled as the two of them exchanged a handshake. While Jeffrey had many friends, Blaine was the one guy I felt good about, and didn't mind introducing Cassie to.

Cassie didn't really seem impressed or even act as if she noticed the man was drop-dead gorgeous and a specimen worth looking at twice. Heck, Blaine deserved a third or fourth look. I knew Marco had it going on back in the day, and that there was a chance that he remained a heartbreaker, but there was a roughneck type of edge to him that Blaine was the complete opposite of. I wasn't sure what Cassie's marriage was like, but I couldn't help wishing that she was available to check Blaine out.

"Hello. It's very nice to meet you." Cassie returned her attention to me. "Aunt Debbie doesn't want anything else to eat. I'm just going to get her a bottle of water and get her situated for bed." She walked to the refrigerator and pulled out a bottle of chilled water.

Out the corner of my eye I could see Blaine watching Cassie's every move. This was so different. In the five years I'd known him, I had never seen him look at any woman more than once, and that was always in a friendly, sister-in-faith kind of way.

Cassie walked around the counter and smiled. "Blaine, it was nice to meet you. Zee, I'm sure I will see you soon." Then she looked at me. "Gabby, will I talk to you before you leave?"

"Oh, definitely." I didn't know what to say. Cassie was controlling the room, and all eyes were on her, to see what she was going to say or do next.

"Where is Alexis?" I asked.

"She's with Aunt Debbie," Cassie said. "If you don't mind, I think she's going to stay with us tonight, you know, help me get settled and used to where everything is."

"Not a problem. I was going to suggest that. We'll talk about church tomorrow morning."

"Okay." She turned and walked out of the room, with less twist than the previous exit, but it was enough bounce to keep Blaine following her with his eyes.

Jeffrey walked in. "Blaine, man. I thought I heard your voice. Come on in and help me make fun of Nate and Todd losing their money."

"That's exactly what I came to do." Blaine laughed. "You'd think these guys would learn. If you ladies will excuse me."

"Of course. Go do what you do." I narrowed my eyes at Jeffrey.

"Boo, I'm just an alpha male." He winked.

"Man, I'm a little tired," I said to Zee after everyone left the room. I cleared my throat. "Almost every bone in my body is achy."

I hadn't said a word to anyone, but I had been feeling out of sorts for a while way before Ms. Emma left town and my schedule doubled with the demands of home and caring for my Mom and her household. When things slowed down and got to a point of almost normal, I planned to make an appointment to see if there was any concern behind my aches and pains, or if it all stemmed from stress. Lord knows, it was the culprit of many illnesses for so many women, and while I rehashed that theory daily to many of my patients, I didn't plan on being ignorant to my own advice.

"I'm a little exhausted myself." Zee rubbed up and down her left arm gingerly and looked around the room. "Everything is in its place, and the kitchen and dining room are back together. Listen, I'm going to go home. Tell Ma Debbie I'll see her at church tomorrow. That's if I feel up to making it. Suddenly, I need a *me* day."

"Oh, okay."

Usually Zee would have expressed some concern over me

saying that I wasn't feeling exactly great. And not often did she miss church. Plus, her *me* days usually were *me* and *Gabby* days. She was still upset, and all I wanted was for her to get over it. Cassie was going to be here for a while, and I didn't plan on having a tense relationship with Zee the entire time.

"Thanks for all your help and for last night. I truly appreciate it." There was no denying that I appreciated Zee. My anger from earlier was completely gone, and she just really needed to follow suit. I couldn't stress it enough because the last thing I needed was to go through a verbal exchange like the one that had already gone down.

"Don't mention it." Zee closed the distance between us, smiled slightly, and kissed my cheek.

The kiss held none of its usual warmth, but before I could press or try to erase the tension that suddenly stood between us like an invisible vapor, she was out the door. Maybe that was for the best. I wasn't sure I had the energy to even ask or suggest. With the exclusion of Zee not being totally in love with the newest of circumstances, this was the highest high I'd had in a very long time.

This wasn't going to be easy, but I knew it would work out. It just had to. I had waited all these years for her to return, and now that she was here, I prayed the petty differences between Zee and her would disappear. Cassie had been a trooper and even in her response, she was cool. Overall, I'd rate tonight at 7, and that was much more than I expected.

I leaned my back against the coolness of the granite countertop and sipped from a cold bottle of flavored water. The tightness in my neck and shoulder muscles was still there. I needed something to take the edge off of what I was feeling. I sighed, just thinking of resorting to medicine to soothe what I should be able to control myself.

While there were noises in the distance, I was all alone here for a second. I took a minute to recall the joyous noises that filled the kitchen earlier. For a fleeting moment I remembered what the kitchen looked like during my youth, almost a lifetime before Mom redecorated and renovated everything. But, more than the décor, I recalled the sounds in this very room during my youth. My smile dropped, and I felt a sharp pain between my shoulders. This house was the same and different at the same time, and somehow I still needed to make sense of it all, but right now I couldn't. I wouldn't.

I pulled myself from the moment and listened as the guys yelled and cheered for their respective teams. I wasn't sure how they could hear each other above the outburst whenever there was something to get loud about. It was a man thing, and this female couldn't relate at all.

I could also faintly hear Cassie and Alexis laughing and engaging Mom in some California story. It all sounded like music to my ears, and reminded me warmly of the sounds of a real-life family. The blended emotion made me smile.

Chapter 9

Cassandra

There was no use prolonging the inevitable. I would have to leave the security of the ladies' room and go into the sanctuary sooner or later. My preference would be later than soon. The problem was, I hadn't been to Mt. Calvary Baptist in forever. Not just Mt. Calvary, I hadn't stepped foot in any place of worship since I'd played grown and left the comfort of home and all that was familiar way back when.

Oakland had churches all over the place, plenty of denominations, any congregational size you wanted, and whatever side of town you wanted it to be on. It was a smorgasbord, and you could truly have it your way. Everywhere you turned, there were signs and advertisements saying they were open and in the business of saving souls. The airwaves were full of broadcasts, and local stations gave Sunday morning airtime to the area's heavy hitters. I'd turn the channels, telling myself that church was a corporate event, that it wouldn't benefit me, an audience of one. Whenever I listened to their spiel, I'd say many of the televangelists had one agenda and one agenda only, money.

I'd actually come close to entering a few churches, querying some of the nurses at the hospital about their church services, the esteemed bishops, pastors, and those responsible for leading the flock, but never followed through. A handful of Sunday mornings, I woke up earlier, determined that

that day would be my turnaround point, that I'd return to my roots and back to salvation and back to a relationship with God, but somewhere between home and my destination, I'd change my mind. Why, I was never really sure. Church hadn't caused me to be callous. Nothing ever happened there that would cause me to feel the way I did. And, heavens, I grew up in the home of a pastor, so I knew what it was like to be an almost-adopted PK.

The underlying reason was much deeper than I even knew, and even though I didn't want to face it directly or indirectly, it was attached to Aunt Debbie and the man she called her husband. It was about what I wanted her to know. If she was the great servant she professed to be, why didn't she know? And why didn't she say something? So, I wasn't mad at religion or the church, just bitter about how I ended up where I did.

I stood gazing in the bathroom mirror of the ladies' room, conveniently nestled in the right corner of the large, spacious vestibule. With every hair in place, my less-is-more makeup job didn't look half bad.

Getting up in the wee hours of the morning before the sun even came up was the easy part, considering the time difference and my schedule being three hours off. Day one had me settling into a routine without any major problem. I had no trouble at all helping Aunt Debbie get showered and dressed. She nodded her approval of the outfit Alexis picked out. Alexis told me it was something Gabby had picked out a few weeks before.

As any good caregiver would assure, we were seated at the breakfast table with a spread that included turkey bacon, turkey sausage, French toast, and home fries. The carafe was full of orange juice, and Aunt Debbie's teacup was full of her favorite herbal blend. I was truly doing it up and had to pinch myself at how well it was all going.

Alexis and Jay high-fived each other after they finished eating and asked that I promise to stay forever. Rubbing their stomachs, they told Gabby they were too full to go to church when she waltzed through the back door dressed to the nines. As I watched her buzz around talking a mile a minute, I wondered if she wore the first thing she picked out, or if she had several outfits stretched across the bed.

I had a number of outfits all over the room upstairs. It was a chore for me to dress for a place I hadn't been in the entire length of my time away. I finally settled on a simple midnight blue wrap dress, a pair of black slings, and neutral color hose. I was almost out the door when I realized I wasn't wearing any jewelry. So I added pearl studs and two strings of pearl beads. Then it was out the room and down the steps.

"Well, good morning, Cassandra," a deep voice greeted me from behind.

I was already familiar with Jeffrey's voice, since we had already exchanged greetings, so I knew it wasn't him. I silently prayed it wasn't Nate or Todd. On the way over, Gabby had described them to me as regular "church-girl hunters," who prayed each Sunday that it would be the Sunday they'd meet the one, and reduce their attendance to occasionally when it suited them.

I turned around and immediately came face to face with the man with the deep voice. "Good morning." I tilted my head to take in his full height.

"Glad to have you join us this morning." He was still smiling.

In the distance two ladies were greeting people who were coming in. They seemed really happy to be about their hospitality business and they proudly wore the badge with honor. I don't remember greeters at the doors, so this had to be one of those new additions toward church harmony and growth.

"Thank you." I couldn't think of anything else to say. *Was I supposed to say, "Glad to be here?"* "Well, I better go on in. Gabby is probably looking for me."

He looked at me, as if disappointed that I didn't continue the conversation for a few more minutes. "I need to get on in myself. I was just checking on the guys that handle our parking lot ministry."

"Oh, okay." I started to move but realized that he was actually blocking the door. I didn't want to walk around him.

He noticed it and smiled. "I'm sorry. Here, let me get the door." He pushed one side of the door open, allowing me to walk in. "I'll see you later."

I turned for a second and managed a smile. It wasn't that hard to smile at him, since he was a very attractive man. I couldn't help but notice, though, that for some reason, I made him nervous. It definitely wasn't that kind of attraction, and I would've been flattered if he thought I was cute. But it probably had more to do with me being related to his friend. Who knows, maybe Jeffrey asked that he be nice to me. I couldn't read anything else in to it. After all, I was supposed to be a happily married woman.

The congregation was still small enough that everything and everybody got immediate attention. I walked down the aisle toward where Gabby, Alexis, and Jay were sitting. I felt like all eyes were on me. Out of the corner of my eye I saw a few older women, about Aunt Debbie's age, point and whisper. I tried to smile.

The pew I was trying to get to seemed so far away. With each pew I passed, the whispers and stares increased. I could see Aunt Debbie's wheelchair pulled beside the front pew.

She sat upright, her head angled, her hat in place and she listened attentively to an elderly lady sitting next to her.

I sat down beside Gabby after squeezing past a few people. I exhaled.

"Are you okay?" Gabby looked over at me, concern all over her face.

"I'm fine. It's just that . . ."

She leaned closer toward me. "It's what?"

"It seems everybody is looking at me."

Just as the words escaped from my lips, Jeffrey and Blaine came out one of the doors toward the side of the sanctuary and sat down in the raised seating next to the pulpit. This must have been Gabby's usual seat, because they both quickly looked in our direction. While Jeffrey's expression was sober, Blaine smiled real wide, as if posing for some camera crew. At least that's what I saw.

I definitely couldn't say the smile was for me or pertained to me. I was just coming on the scene and didn't know the man from Adam and surely couldn't vouch for his church etiquette, so I immediately dismissed it. The man was probably looking at someone behind us or maybe in the few pews in front of where we were seated. After all with its complete facelift, the church was no longer the small edifice I remembered. It looked very similar to the sanctuaries I saw on television right before I flipped the channel.

"They probably are. Girl, you know this is still a small country church, and everything and everybody is news. We've grown in size, and of course it looks all different, up-to-date and state-of-the-art." Gabby looked all around her, as if taking me on a quick visual tour. "But it's still the same. By the time service is over, someone will have recognized you and spread the word that Aunt Debbie's niece, Cassie, is in town." Then she added, "You just need to be glad that Mom can't serve as church crier. She would be at the pulpit telling the story of the Prodigal Son, of course, renaming the main character *Cassandra*."

"Ain't that the truth."

Here I was, back home, my tail tucked between my legs. It wasn't so much to assist, but more along the lines of not knowing what to do with the rest of my broke life. If I had stayed in Oakland, I could have only floated so long before my financial boat sunk.

"Well, well . . . if it isn't the prodigal daughter . . ."

We looked up to see Zee slide in the pew past three elderly women and a little girl to take a seat right next to me. Obviously, no one clued her that all outfits should be chosen with enough room to breathe. Her tan suit was so snug, I was sure she could only take a few quick breaths in intervals. I didn't even want to think about what would happen if she had to bend over, or if a fire broke out and she had to make a mad dash out of here. And her wide-brimmed brown hat was sure to block everyone's vision three or four pews back.

"Good morning, Gabby. Don't you look nice this morning. Child, that dress is beautiful." Zee glanced around as if she hadn't insulted me. "My, my, Ma Debbie is looking sharp as a tack this morning." She leaned over, hitting me in the face with her hat. "Gabby, isn't that the outfit we picked out?"

Gabby bucked her eyes in disbelief. She gave Zee a stern look of disapproval. "Yes, it is. And why are you leaning all across Cassie with that wide-behind hat on? You come breezing in here on a whirlwind like a black Scarlett O'Hara."

I wanted to burst out laughing at Gabby's remark, but I was still ticked at Zee for calling me the prodigal daughter. Sure, me and Gabby had just joked about it, but she wasn't included in our inside joke, and I had never given her the green light to joke me about anything. I wasn't going to have it.

"My, Zee, you look *extra* nice today." I put a lot of emphasis on the word *extra*, hoping she got the hint. My eyes locked with hers, and I never blinked or turned away. She needed to know that I could give as good as I get. I'd never been a pushover and while I had mellowed tremendously, I was still one that stood my ground.

"Thanks . . . I think." She rolled her eyes and settled back in the pew, with a sudden interest in the Sunday bulletin.

"You're so welcome." I smiled a sugary sweet smile, and turned slightly right before winking at Gabby. I didn't want to use too much energy to deal with her attitude and antics. Right now I needed to find my way around what used to be home and put the pieces of my life back together.

"Oh, praise and worship is about ready to start, and you don't want Mom to catch us talking," Gabby said.

"I remember those days all too well," I said, thinking of the way Aunt Debbie would glance over her shoulder at us and not turn back around until we closed our pre-service conversation.

The service was very moving, and Reverend Frank Douglass seemed to be a great preacher. That's all I could say, since I wasn't an authority on preachers and I didn't have anyone to compare him to. Although from the minute I settled back to listen to the message, many of Aunt Debbie's sermons flowed through my mind and I could envision her standing in the very place he stood.

A fancy lectern of wood and acrylic replaced the one I remembered. The pulpit had been expanded, and Aunt Debbie was no longer beckoning whosoever to come on and give their burdens to the Lord, as if her very life depended on it. I'd watch as tears flowed from her eyes and streamed down the sides of her face.

Watching Rev. Douglass do the same caused something within me to twist up. I suddenly became flushed and felt sick.

There must have been a look of panic on my face, because Gabby reached over and squeezed my hand.

I squeezed back. "I think I need to get some water." To avoid alerting Zee that there was a problem, I exited the pew on the other side.

The usher assigned to our section led the way to the back of the sanctuary and opened the door for me. I tried not to run or push her out of my way, but she was moving with all the speed of a snail. Once I got outside the doors, I exhaled and held my chest as a sharp pain hit me.

"Are you okay?" Blaine was standing beside me and had placed a hand on my back.

"I'm okay. Must have been something I ate for breakfast." I was almost sure it wasn't anything I ate, but I couldn't tell him that I panicked and had to rush out for another reason.

"Look, I'm going to get Gabby and have her take you home. I'm sure Jeffrey can handle getting Pastor Taylor home."

"That won't be necessary." When I tried to stand straight, I felt the pain again and immediately returned to my bent-over position. "This is so embarrassing." I tried to chuckle.

Blaine's hand never left my back. When one of the ushers brought a cup of water, he kindly accepted it and told her, "I'll handle everything. Just go in and get Sister Easton."

We walked over to a nearby bench and took a seat. I deep-breathed a few times, and the pain subsided.

"You probably need to go get checked out, just to make sure it's not anything serious."

"Are you a doctor or something?" I was getting irritated. I knew it was anxiety. "I happen to be a nurse and have been for a number of years, so I think I would know if something was more than plain old heartburn or acid reflux." I rolled my eyes up in my head. "Jesus Christ."

Blaine looked as if I had punched him in the stomach. "I'm not a doctor, and I'm so sorry. I was suggesting that something more than that could be wrong. I was just thinking you should go as a cautionary measure. And, yes, Jeffrey did mention you were a nurse."

By the time he had finished his apology, I was feeling awful for going off on him.

"Cassie, are you okay?" Gabby was charging in our direction.

"I'm fine. If you could take me back to Aunt Debbie's, that would be great. I just need to rest up a little. It's nothing but heartburn."

"Oh, okay." She looked like she wanted to believe that's all it was. "Let me bring the car around."

"Girl, that's overboard. I can walk to the car with you." I stood up. This time I wasn't thrown back into a bent-over position.

Gabby turned to Blaine. "Thanks. I appreciate you giving Cassie a hand."

"It was no problem at all. If you can manage, and I think you can, I'll go on back inside. I had only come out to get something from the media room for Rev. Douglass."

"Okay." Gabby looked a little confused at his hasty departure. "Well, as I said, I appreciate you."

"Sure." He threw his hand up and continued to walk down the nearby hallway, never even bothering to say good-bye to me.

But why should he? I was a terror. I was sure that was our last conversation. There would be no need for him to touch my back, reminding me that I was supposed to be married. Yet, for more reasons than one, I was wishing I didn't have to pretend.

Chapter 10

Gabrielle

I walked into the steam-filled bathroom and listened as Jeffrey hummed a tune, my mouth curved in a slight smile. The kids were still asleep, and our suite was off-limits to them when the door was closed. Not wanting to miss the opportunity right before me, I removed the oversized tee shirt I wore, something I did often, and he'd always enjoyed every minute of it. Until lately.

Now, he seemed so pre-occupied with issues that he didn't bother to share. Whatever it was on his mind, I was an outsider frantically trying to mentally tap in, and I was coming up empty.

My reflection in the lighted mirror didn't look half-bad. Of course, like many women, I worried that he just wasn't attracted to me anymore. Along with age came a change to the body that the best of care and careful pampering couldn't avert, so I'd worked extra hard, and wanted to believe the additional workouts I was indulging in with Zee and, occasionally, Cassie were paying off.

I pulled the curtain back and looked at Jeffrey's lathered body. The aroma of his body wash was so inviting. "Can I join you?"

A look of shock came over his face. He wiped at his eyes and blinked a few times to get the soap out. "Well, I was getting ready to get out."

I stepped in the shower, which was big enough for two, and eased up behind him. We had shower sprays positioned on two sides of the shower wall, and those directly behind me released strong streams of water against my back. When our bodies touched, I felt a sensation ripple below my navel.

"Now, I'm going to ask again. Can I join you?"

"You can, but I'm not really in the mood for anything to happen." He continued to rinse off his body under the sprays of warm water.

"I'd like a second opinion." Just as I was getting ready to touch him, he turned around, completely out of my reach. "Why are you turning around?" I started laughing, hoping this was just a game he was playing. I reached around him and tried to remove the washcloth he held over his private area.

"Gabrielle, stop playing. I'm not in the mood," he repeated, his voice a little louder than I thought it should be.

I looked up as he moved his head and a spray of water hit my face. Without saying a word or searching his face for an explanation, I turned and got out of the shower.

By the time he dried off and came into our bedroom, I was getting dressed for work. I busied around the room, not really wanting him to see the hurt on my face.

"Gabrielle, don't take it personal. I'm just not in the mood. It's not you, it's me." He walked toward me and stopped when he was close to where I was standing.

All my inner alarms went off. How could he even say the words so many other men say right before they walk out of a relationship? I had heard it too many times from so many of my clients when they summarized what their mates said right before the end.

I cleared my throat a little. "Okay. Well, I'm going downstairs to fix some breakfast." I leaned against the dresser to put on my shoe. Just as I was about to walk out of our bedroom, I turned around and walked over to where he was. I had to try this. "Can I have a kiss?"

He looked up at me as if confused. In one swift movement, he stood up and kissed me on the forehead.

I didn't want to chance speaking, didn't want to explode. All I could do was turn around and walk out.

"We have a code of conduct to uphold here, and I'm really disappointed that you've shown so little regard for your co-worker and the privacy of the clients here at the center." Dr. Johns looked over her small-framed glasses at Terry.

We had only been in the meeting for ten minutes, and it was already coming to a close. She didn't handle staff relations much because our human resources division handled many of those details for her, but this was something that she just had to step in on. From the first time I shared my concern with her, she was adamant about preventing another event of this sort.

Rather than argue the point, Terry admitted that she might have inadvertently shared some information that she'd over-heard.

Dr. Johns added, "I have high regard for Mrs. Easton's professionalism, and she has always supported you to the utmost. I can't see why you would share any conversation that you heard directly, let alone, indirectly."

"I know, Dr. Johns. I was completely out of order. I have submitted a formal apology to Mrs. Easton."

"That is all well and good, but that doesn't erase the harm done at your careless sharing." Dr. Johns stood up and placed a letter on formal letterhead in front of Terry. "I have a few options, according to Human Resources, and since you've already taken care of the formal apology, I'm also suspending you from all services here at the center for three days."

"What?" Terry stood up. "The letter of apology should be enough."

"Are you telling me how to run my center?" Dr. Johns came back around the desk she had just circled. She wasn't a small woman by any stretch of the imagination. In fact, she towered over most and had to be close to six feet.

Her coming back around the conference table and positioning herself within inches of Terry had to cause her to think that maybe, just maybe, she should have thought before her outburst. My eyes were wide as if watching an attacker and its prey. This was close to something straight off a National Geographic episode.

"No, I'm not." Terry returned to her seat. She signed her name at the bottom of the letter and pushed it to the center of the table. "If you don't mind, I have one more appointment for today, and I will need to make arrangements for the next three days."

"I suggest that you think seriously about this turn of events and take your position as a member of our team more seriously. I know there are a few busybodies in the building, but I expect you, not only as a staff member, but as a counselor, to deal with them in a nondestructive way. Bits of information about our clients and or staff hurt not just them and you, but the center as a whole."

"Fine." She got up from the table. "Gabrielle, I'm sorry," she said, leaving the office.

"Apology accepted." I couldn't really give her a visual expression of my acceptance because my face would not support what I didn't really feel just yet. I was all about forgiving and forgetting and that was indeed my nature. I just needed to be real. This would take time.

Dr. Johns fell in her seat. "I don't care how long I've been in management, I can never get used to reprimanding an employee." She took a sip from the can of ginger ale on her desk.

"I'm sorry you had to take care of that, and I'm sorry I had to bring the situation to you in the first place." I really did hate having to share this with my boss, but if I didn't, it could've happened to someone else.

"That's so true."

Dr. Johns answered her phone. "Yes, Pat. Oh, I'll tell her." She returned her phone back to the cradle and directed her attention back to me. "That was a reminder call for you. Your three o'clock is here."

"Oh, dag! I lost track of time." I stood up. "Thanks again for your help with this."

"Don't mention it. Let me know if you have any more problems."

The minute I got to my office, my personal line was ringing. "Gabrielle Easton."

"What time do you plan on getting home?" Jeffrey asked, no hello or any other kind expression.

For the past two weeks, Jeffrey was up and down with me. One minute he was warm and sensitive, the next, he didn't have much to say and was totally evasive. For Cassie and Mom, he put on a good face, and they saw us as okay. But I knew something was out of order.

We didn't argue in front of the kids. I'd quickly defused the situation, and allow him his way over whatever we were at odds about. We'd kept the marital bed warm on occasion. Then Jeffrey went to climbing on top of me and it was over. All without a kiss. That bothered me the most.

"I'm planning on being on time. I got to stop at the market, and then I'll be home." I sighed as I leaned back in the swivel chair.

An old photo of Jeffrey and I, the smiling faces of two people holding on to each other tightly, was situated on the corner of my desk. It was from a gala we had attended. I closed my eyes and thought about that night we'd made passionate love on the living room floor, not able to make it to our second-floor bedroom. The kids had both left for overnight visits, so we were all alone. We had laughed afterward, joking that we were much too old to be replaying scenes from our youth. Neither one of us could get out of the bed the next morning.

"I was just checking. I never know with you. I'll be late. The boss has called a late meeting, and then we're planning to hit the sports bar for wings and to catch the game together."

It was all a just-for-your-information kind of sharing. It truly didn't sound like he was asking for my opinion or my approval. I really wanted to ask why he decided an impromptu outing with his coworkers and friends, when we usually made arrangements like that together after making sure the other had no plans that involved the other.

"Oh, okay. Well, the kids and I will have dinner, and I'll do a few things around the house. I don't need to physically check on Mom and Cassie. I was over there for lunch."

"Well, I'll see you later. Got to go."

There was a knock on the door. "Come in."

Pat, one of the young interns, leaned her head around the door. "Mrs. Easton, did you remember that Mrs. Gates is here."

"Dag! I'm sorry. Please ask her to come in."

How was I going to concentrate on this session? My mind was selfishly on my own problems. Needing therapy myself, how could I help some other poor married woman make sense of why her husband wore feminine undergarments on Sundays? Just Sundays, no other day of the week. He told her that he equated the wonderful feel of silk against his skin with being totally free, and that the Sabbath, being a rest day, was the ideal day for such freeness.

Just when you think your situation is bad, someone else comes along with a bigger problem.

I recalled Dr. Johns telling me that her door was always open. She had even said it again after our meeting with Terry. It was something in her eyes that touched me enough to consider talking to her about my own problems. While I didn't want to discuss my affairs in-house, she was at the top, and maybe, just maybe, talking to her would help me in some way, and she would still respect my ability to handle other people's affairs.

There had to be somebody that could help me make sense of why my husband wouldn't kiss me, why the intimacy we had always known was gone. The quick brush against my cheek in the morning wasn't what I considered a decent good-bye kiss. Even when I cornered him, or put my face directly in front of his, he'd turn away or come up with something to avoid the closeness.

I stared at the photo that held our likeness and pictured Jeffrey in something frilly and sexy. I even visually changed the color from black to red, and back to black from red, gauging what would best complement his complexion.

I busted out laughing and said out loud, "Never that."

Just then, Mrs. Gates tapped lightly and opened my door. She stood inside the door with her usual easygoing appeal. Her silver hair in place, she was the ideal image of a grandmotherly person. In fact, the week before she had just turned sixty-five, and had mentioned to me that Mr. Gates was seventy.

Imagine a seventy-year-old man in a few of Vickie's pieces. I concealed my laughter, placing the file folder I was holding up to my mouth.

Chapter 11

Cassandra

"Aunt Debbie, as soon as we finishing eating and I do the dishes, I think we should play a little bingo."

I pushed my chair back from the table and picked up my plate. The grilled chicken and spinach salad was very filling. We completed our well-balanced and healthy dinner with a fattening piece of homemade pound cake covered with fresh strawberries and whip cream. It sort of defeated our light dinner entrée, but neither of us could resist the temptation.

The past two weeks were consumed with meal planning, grocery shopping, pharmacy pickups, physical therapy visits, and other outings. There were days we'd go to the park, visit some of her friends, or just do a little window-shopping. It was all a part of my therapeutic plan for Aunt Debbie. The only place I hadn't taken her and hadn't been in the past two weeks was the church.

The first Sunday after I went, I complained of a headache. When Bible study night came around, I had cramps. By the following Sunday I was back to the cramps. And Aunt Debbie had a slight cold last night and wasn't feeling up to going. So, creativity in the exaggeration department had been working, although I knew time would run out and I'd have to go back.

In my short period of time back home and being totally devoted to taking care of her, I could tell she was beginning to trust me. Up until this point, she'd exercised her right and rejected efforts to get her speech back by having a speech thera-pist come in and work with her. Something inside, along with my experience with older people in similar medical condi-tions, told me it was time to call the speech therapist back in and work on getting her to talk. While she didn't support my thought with anything concrete, her attention to everything I said, and physical responses through nods, eye movements, and hand gestures were telling me something else. No matter how much I talked and how many times I asked her to try to say something she wouldn't, but the gestures were always there, and the nods were on point. I had worked with too many stroke victims to give up, and I knew by the progress she was making with physical therapy and rehabilitation that her speech should easily be restorable as well, she just had to be willing. And for some reason, Aunt Debbie wasn't.

There was a knock on the door just as we settled in to play bingo. "I wonder who that is. Gabby didn't say she was com-ing." I looked at Aunt Debbie, and she nodded, confirming that Gabby hadn't said anything about coming.

The knock came from the back door, which meant that the person was a regular visitor and felt comfortable enough to come around to the back of the house. Anyone else, even Jehovah Witnesses for that matter, all announced themselves by knocking or ringing the bell at the front door, giving the occupant of the house the opportunity to glance out some window to see who was there, and quickly close the curtain before the caller could see them and realize that someone was indeed home.

I'd never thought much about the tactics of the Witnesses, until I moved to Oakland and realized that they were every-where, and all of them, regardless of what coast they were on, had the same agenda, to get into your home and place their magazines in your hand, and to request if they can return at a later time to talk their talk. I had mistakenly answered the

business, which was doing quite well. He had incorporated a training and certification program in his business and actually formally trained many of the young men he employed, who before then were unemployable. He had been, as Gabby put it, a saving grace for many guys who would have turned to selling drugs, doing drugs, or ended up in jail. That part touched me as I thought about Marco, how he could have ended up if someone had reached out to help him make better of his life. All of what she shared made me wonder how old Blaine was. He couldn't have been as young as he looked and accomplished all that he had.

I swear, I thought the girl got ESP or just plain God-given discernment because the minute I thought it, she said, "I hear you. He's fifty-five."

I mentally did the math, he was sixteen years my senior. Would I even date someone that much older than me? I had actually paused to think about it, but I had to remind myself for the umpteenth time that I was supposed to be married. This was getting so hard to remember.

One day I'd received all this mail in the name of Cassandra Price, and when Gabby flipped through it on the way from the mailbox, she immediately asked why I'd never used my married name. I did a quick modern-woman, family-connection song and dance, and she along with a silent Aunt Debbie bought it. What I needed to figure out was how to dissolve a non-existent marriage, not because of Blaine by any means—It wasn't that type of party—but just because I knew I needed to.

"Cassandra, do you think I can come in and give them to her, or is she taking a nap?" Blaine asked.

"Huh?" Still holding the door, I had been looking at his lips but had missed what he said.

"Can I come in and give them to her, or is she asleep?" He tried saying the same thing in a different way.

"Oh, sure. I'm sorry." I was embarrassed. I moved away

from the door, and he came in. "She's in the family room. We were just playing bingo." I followed him. "Oh, do you want something to drink?" I was trying to rebound from stumbling on stupid minutes before. How could I just stand there staring at the man like he was a ham hock or a smoked turkey leg with collard greens on the side and a big ol' piece of cornbread? I equated Blaine to food because ever since I landed, I had been eating good, down-home, Southern country cooking whenever the church ladies dropped off food to Aunt Debbie, and that was usually every day. I had to be careful and remind myself with every bite that there was a time when I was really overweight. As much as I was enjoying it all, I didn't want to risk overdoing it.

Blaine paused and turned around. "I'd love something."

"Oh, okay." I was staring again and tried to play it off by clearing my throat. "I have iced tea with lemon. Is that okay?"

"Sounds great."

"You can go on in and have a seat. I'll get the pitcher of iced tea and a few glasses. Aunt Debbie may want a little something to wet her whistle."

I waited until he was around the corner and out of immediate view. If I could kick my own butt, I would have. The man had caused me to make the biggest fool of myself. I didn't understand my own actions. I was so cool the first time I'd met him. And the second time, well, I was a complete hellion, and today I stood before him a mumbling, blundering foul.

The man must think I'm bipolar. I busied myself with getting a tray and putting the tea in the flowered glass pitcher and pulling out the glasses that matched it.

Just before I carried the tray in, I took the time to cut a piece of cake, topped it with some strawberries, and a dash of whipped cream. I wasn't sure if he indulged in sweets, but I figured I'd take a chance.

A little deep breathing and hopefully this time around,

I wouldn't make a fool of myself. Right before I entered the family room, I stood in the hallway and listened as he talked to Aunt Debbie. He carried on a conversation as if it was two-way. While she understood everything everyone said completely, it was challenging to carry on a one-way conversation, and yet we all did so to keep her stimulated. I couldn't help but smile as he talked and laughed.

"Here we go."

Blaine stood up and removed the tray I was carrying. "Oh, my! Is that Southern pound cake? I had just asked Pastor Taylor if there had been some baking in the house today when I picked up on the aroma of vanilla and nutmeg."

I chuckled. "So you know a little about baking, or is it just the smells?" I had to give him a few cool points for knowing a little something about distinctive cooking aromas.

"Both. I love to cook. Don't get a chance to do it often since there is no one to cook for, but when the kids come over, I dabble a little, and everyone leaves with a smile on their face and no stomachaches."

"Well, that's you telling the story. I'll have to check out the facts." I was still standing looking at him.

Blaine placed the wooden tray on the corner of the coffee table, looking back at me. For a moment I had forgotten that Aunt Debbie was even in the room. There had to be something he had done since the last time I saw him. Some cologne or fragrance he'd put on had my senses reeling.

"You don't have to go far. I've cooked for Pastor Taylor a time or two throughout the years, and I'm sure she can tell you that it wasn't half-bad."

Blaine looked down at Aunt Debbie in her wheelchair, her lap covered with a lightweight cloth, since she always seemed to get a chill this time of evening, even though it was spring and the weather was beautiful outside. As nice as the weather is in California, this season was so beautiful in my hometown.

Aunt Debbie reached for Blaine's hand, and he allowed her to place it between her two. She rubbed it, looking up at me and nodding in the positive with a crooked smile.

"See. I believe, Ms. Cassandra that means yes."

I couldn't help but pick up on the detail of being referred to as Ms. I wondered if anyone had bothered to tell him I was married. I just wondered how much Gabby had told him about me. It was something for me to wonder about, since I was introduced to him the same way I was to everyone else, Cassandra Price.

No one ever asked about Marco. Not even Gabby or Jeffrey mentioned his name or questioned about the details of my marriage. It went without a doubt that my extended stay would leave a husband beyond who called daily. The times they had been at the house, not one phone call came through on the house phone for me, and not often did they even see me on my cellular phone. The only person that brought his name up a few times was Zee, and that was to point out the obvious, that I had run away with a hoodlum, who was likely still a hoodlum. Her point was, if that described him to a tee, what did that make me?

"Well, Aunt Debbie wouldn't steer me wrong, so I'm going to have to believe her." I poured the ice tea in the glasses and put one foot in front of the other, until I was in the side chair beside Aunt Debbie.

Blaine sat down on the sofa across from us. He sipped his tea and held up the glass with a smile. "That is really good."

"I won't take any credit for brewing it. I was able to take a shortcut, thanks to Nestea." I chuckled.

"Well, I know people who can't make a good glass of instant tea, so take the compliment."

The one thing I noticed about Mr. Blaine was, he had no trouble handing out compliments, and there was always a smile on his face, and a look of totally being relaxed and comfortable.

I pushed the dessert plate with the cake and fresh strawberries toward him. "Here you might as well make a comparison, and then maybe we can exchange a few recipes."

Again I noticed how nice he looked even dressed down. I was going to make sure that for the reminder of my stay I was dressed decent. That was one thing I had forgotten, living in a pastoral house meant that company came often, and usually without an invitation, another of the things that hadn't changed.

"Pastor Taylor was pointing out that you two were about to play bingo. I'd love to stay and play if you don't mind."

"I'm sure you have more important things to do than play bingo with us. This is one of our evening rituals." I nervously played with the bingo cards and tried to avoid looking at him.

"Contrary. I have nothing else to do for the rest of the evening. I'm completely open, and I'd like nothing better than to hang out with you two beautiful ladies."

"Aunt Debbie, he must be talking to you . . . 'cause I look a mess. I wasn't expecting any visitors, as you probably guessed."

I looked down at my sweats and the many holes that ran through the worn fabric. They just happened to be my favorite, and the more holes they got, the more comfortable they were. There were sections where you could see more flesh than fabric, and that had never bothered me until now. But then I never really entertained guests in my home and didn't really spend time hanging out that much. My evening company was usually just the television, a little music, and whatever food I chose to soothe the misery of being hurt and alone.

The hurt stayed with me for so long, I never really knew what it was like to wake up and not feel empty and hollow. It's hard to be alone under normal circumstances, but when you decide that it's the best course of action for self-betterment, what should be a moderate transition is sometimes real hard. Getting over what you gave up for a better you can still be a difficult task and cuts just as deep.

"There is nothing wrong with relax gear. I think everyone has a few pairs just like the ones you have on. I know I do, not to mention, in the signature color of gray. Now, if you tell me you have a pair in that color, I'll know you're the real deal and not all phony and uptight."

I couldn't help but laugh along with him as I looked over at Aunt Debbie, who was shaking her head. "I do, and trust me there is nothing uptight about me. I'm just as real as the next person." I thought about my make-pretend marriage.

"I'm glad to hear that. In fact, you know what? A client of mine gave me three tickets to the gospel play Saturday evening, and I can't think of any two people I'd rather take than you and Pastor Taylor. Besides, it's been a while since me and Pastor Taylor took in a play. I can't even remember the last time."

"I can't believe that. I'm sure there are women waiting in line to hang out with you, and a few of them probably have a mother or an aunt who could tag along."

I couldn't believe he was asking us. More like asking Aunt Debbie. Again, this likely had nothing to do with me. Gabby did say he was a hot commodity at the church and in the community, telling me how all the single or widowed women were all but throwing their lace drawers at him, and to their disappointment, he wouldn't bite. Instead of giving up, many of them stepped up their game, determined to be the next Mrs. Blaine Warner.

"That may be true. But Pastor Taylor is dear to me, and I'm sure you could use a nice evening out. To be honest, Cassandra, I'd love to reintroduce you to your hometown."

I wondered again, *Does he know I'm married?*

Aunt Debbie looked at me, tapped my leg twice, and pointed to Blaine.

"I think she's saying that we accept." When I glanced back at her, she put her thumb up a little.

"It's a date then," Blaine said confidently. "Wait." He placed another piece of cake on his fork and put it in his mouth. He closed his eyes, savoring the flavor. "This is delicious. Cassandra, I tip my hat to you. We're exchanging recipes, starting tomorrow."

I was flattered. "Yeah, right. I think you're just pulling my leg." I watched as he chewed and acted as if it was mouthwatering.

"Not at all. Now that I know you are a better baker, let's see if you are any good at the game of bingo."

"Yeah, let's see. Me and Aunt Debbie are going to beat your butt and send you on home." I laughed, and it actually felt good.

Aunt Debbie patted my hand gently and pointed at Blaine, confirming that we were about to wipe the floor with him.

"Child, bingo is an old man's game. I was playing bingo like a pro when you were still in pampers with cute little pigtails."

His laughter mixed with mine, and I liked the sound of us laughing together. It seemed he was comfortable with not only the skin he was in, which was put together well, from where I was sitting, but also with being older and seasoned.

I caught myself. Why shouldn't he be? He wasn't here to impress or win anyone over by displaying a youthful appeal.

"Maybe so. But wisdom doesn't necessarily come with age these days. Let's just play, and then we'll see. Let me warn you, though, my win comes complete with a victory dance. I normally perform it on the table, but since we're in the company of Pastor Taylor, I'll reserve this section of the floor." I pointed to an area not far from where we were sitting.

Aunt Debbie tapped me on the leg and grunted.

I smiled at my own humor, and also because it wouldn't be long before Aunt Debbie joined our conversations. I didn't broadcast it, but it was the first sound she had made since I'd been home. It was a victory. My experience told me that. I was going to call Gabby as soon as Blaine left and tell her all about it. I didn't want to sound an internal emotional alarm, but I was really hoping he wouldn't be leaving anytime soon.

Then there was Saturday to look forward to, even if it was a threesome. If there was standing room only to get to Mr. Warner, I had suddenly moved to the front of the crowd, even if it was for one night and in the company of Aunt Debbie. I'd rein myself in later. Right now I was in awe at being asked out.

We had just talked about being real, and I was really wondering if what I was seeing was real. God knows, I hadn't had a lot of practice. There was only Marco, and a few guys I went out with, only to try to get over him. The times with someone other than Marco, I could count on one hand, and one of them had been a repeat. Now, here I was in the comfort of my family home with the one person who adored me as I was, flaws and all, and the other who seemed to be looking right at me. Maybe he liked what he was seeing. I didn't need nor want to borrow any worries; I had my share of those, but I could hope, if only for one night.

Chapter 12

Gabrielle

The back of Zee's Land Rover was loaded with shopping bags, and as usual, only one or two of those belonged to me, the others were for Alexis, Jay, and Jeffrey. I had joined Zee on a shopping excursion to the outlets, and as usual the prices were right, and the variety wide. The sound of racks parting, credit cards being swiped, and the cash holders slamming against the crisp bills was all music to my ears. People had their vices, and I had shopping. I didn't do it so often that it left me broke, making materialistic purchases when I should be taking care of the necessities, but every now and then, I enjoyed a good shopping trip. It was always the exercise of choice.

My first instinct was to have one of my mother's friends sit with her for the day and ask Cassie, who was so deserving of a break, to come along. For the past month she had spent every day and night caring for Mom, never complaining and always with a smile on her face. She was so excited when she called to tell me that Mom was actually starting to make noises and grunts. It didn't seem major when I shared it with Jeffrey, but when we called the speech therapist the next day, he confirmed that Mom was starting to take the step needed to speech rehabilitation.

I knew Cassie was going above and beyond, trying to make up for the years she wasn't around. As much as I told her that it was forgotten and forgiven and that no one was keeping a record of wrongs, it seemed she worked that much harder. I assured her that all Mom had ever done was pray that she was safe, happy, and would one day come back home to the people who loved her.

Mom had a direct line, and God had brought her back. The authority Mom said she had it on convinced me to wait patiently for it to all work out. I'd learned that what looked doubtful often became the platform for a miracle.

I didn't feel too bad about this time with Zee, since Cassie and I had gone to dinner and a movie the night before, Jeffrey had to work late, and the kids had a school dance.

"Can you swing by the bookstore when we leave here?" I had a few books on my to-read list.

"Anything for my bestie." Zee maneuvered out of the outlet parking lot. "I can't believe I found the color shirt I needed to match the new slacks I've had in my closet since our last shopping trip. I could do the happy dance just for that."

"Well, go on then." I laughed and slipped on my sunglasses.

Just then a horn sounded, and a car full of young boys pulled up next to us. One of them hollered, "Hey, shortie."

I acted as if I didn't see them. "Zee, who those little macks think they talking to? I'm old enough to be their mommy."

Zee looked at me. "They don't know that. Put down that window and let me see if you still got it."

"Girl, you are crazy. I'm going to continue to look straight ahead and act like I got good sense. Those little boys could be robbers and murderers."

After they sped off, I thought about Jay. I was hoping he wouldn't be hanging out the window, talking about some shortie. Lines had gotten so weak.

We settled in the restaurant just as many other lunchtime guests were coming in. "I'm starved. I didn't eat anything before I left home."

"I'm hungry, and I did eat before I left home." She laughed.

Zee always laughed when she referred to her overeating or her weight. She tried to mask the irritation, but I could tell she was putting on more pounds, and I also knew it was bothering her more than she wanted to let on.

A strawberry blonde young girl bounced over to take our orders. "Good afternoon, ladies. Are you on your way to the outlets, or is the car already loaded down?"

The waitress seemed very happy, and not just your everyday, regular kind of happy but medication-assisted happy. From my occupational training, I could spot something like that a mile away.

"We are just coming from." I smiled. "Can I get a strawberry lemonade, and could we get a blooming onion? We aren't really ready to order our entrees." I smiled back up at her real hard.

"Give me strawberry lemonade as well. And, in addition to the onion, could I get the wings?" Zee's eyes were taking in two guys who had just walked in the restaurant, and whom the hostess was bringing our way.

When the server saw Zee looking in their direction, she asked, "Are they with you two?"

"No," I said.

"Okay then. I'll put your appetizer orders in and be right back with your drinks." Pippy was off.

"Earth to Zenith."

"Oh, yeah. Girl, I'm here just looking around a little." Zee reached in her oversized Coach bag and pulled her makeup bag out and refreshed her lipstick.

"Flash, boo—I don't think you refresh your lipstick until after you've eaten. We are still eating, aren't we?" I giggled.

The voices of the two men carried a little, and I turned around to get a glance, since my lunch date was consumed with them. I had to say they weren't bad looking.

"That was funny. Ha! Ha! You are a regular comedian. I must take you someplace to perform."

"Nope. I keep my humor for the ones I love, those who truly appreciate what I bring to the table."

Pippy was back with the drinks. "Here you go, ladies." She actually sounded like she was from the outback. "You ready to order now?"

"I believe so. Let's see. I'm torn, but I think I'll have the parmesan pasta with grilled shrimp and scallops, and a salad with ranch dressing."

"Very well then." She turned her attention to Zee. "How about you?"

"I'll have the Alice spring chicken and a salad with Italian dressing." Zee handed the menu to Pippy and smiled. "Thanks."

The minute Pippy walked away, I asked, "What happened? I thought you wanted ribs."

"Girl, I'm not trying to mess up and get rib juice and sauce all over my mouth and this man is looking me up and down."

"Oh, I see. So you're depriving yourself because you're being watched?" I narrowed my eyes at her, pointing my pointer finger in her direction.

She pointed back. "Exactly."

Pippy came back to our table with the appetizers and the salads, placed everything before us, and turned to leave.

"Do you think I can bless the food?"

Zee barely heard me, or so it seemed. "Oh, yeah, do the thing."

I blessed the food and began to pull off a piece of the onion.

Zee pushed the wings in my direction.

"What are you doing?"

"Don't want him to think I'm a big eater." She began to nibble at her salad.

"Whatever." I picked up a wing and went for it. "At least I won't be hungry on the way home and have to stop to get a bag of chips."

"I know I'm being silly, but my biological clock is ticking so loud, it wakes me up at night."

"So this is about marriage, and not just getting some." I paused to wipe my mouth with the napkin. I was glad she had ordered the wings, because they were good.

Zee had suddenly become very serious. "Honestly?"

"Honestly."

"I'm ready to have a baby, and I'm planning on doing so with or without a father. It would just make it better if I had someone to be the father."

"So you want to date, get to know each other, have sex, and marry? I mean, are the beginning and latter parts of that going to be left out of the equation?"

"Likely. And don't look at me like that."

"Like what? I'm just trying to make sense of what you're saying."

"This may not be a good time to talk about this. I mean, it's been something I've been thinking about for over six months. And I've already laid the groundwork and taken the first step."

"When? Since we've been in the restaurant?" I thought she was talking about the love connection she was trying to make.

"Seriously, Gabby, hear me out. There are several parts in this that you will need to play."

"Okay." I gave her my attention while feasting on the onion and the wings. I didn't even bother to eat the salad. Who needed rabbit food when I was loading up on the real stuff?

Zee continued to push her salad around. "I'm scheduled

for surgery next week," she said, not even looking up at me, "and I need you to go with me."

"Oh my God! What's wrong? To have the baby?" I threw my hands up in confusion.

I immediately felt bad. We saw each other at work and talked often, but all of my attention had been on Cassie and making her feel at home. And although Zee didn't say so, she knew that's what I was doing.

"There's nothing really wrong. You've known that I've been taking high blood pressure pills, and for the longest I've been borderline diabetic." She looked at me, waiting for me to acknowledge those facts.

"Yes. And I've stayed on you about eating better and even asked—hold up—begged you to go to the gym with me. Because you wouldn't go with me, I've gained weight myself. And you call yourself a friend," I said, trying to make light of everything. What she was telling me was a serious situation, and I knew that, since Mom's stroke, she'd thought that she might be a candidate for one.

"I am. That's why I'm taking steps to take care of myself. I'm not trying to end up with something major and have you care for me. And I'm definitely not trying to take a dirt nap." She paused. "I've decided to have Lap-Band surgery."

"Really?"

"Really. I'm excited about it, and before you try to talk me out of it, my mind is made up. I've done the research, had all the preliminaries done. It's a done deal." Zee was still consumed with Mr. Delicious at the nearby table.

"Well, Ms. Zee, I support you one hundred percent."

By the time we ended our lunch and paid our check, the two guys were finishing up at the same time.

As we stood up to leave, the guy with the dreads that Zee had been having a visual exchange with stood up.

"Excuse me, Miss," he said. "Please forgive me for staring

at you." He smiled and continued. "I think you are a very beautiful sister. Now, I'm not going to come on real strong; that's not my style. And I'm not going to ask for your number, but what I'm going to do is give you mine." He handed her a business card.

The tall bald guy with him handed me his card. "And if you don't mind, pretty lady, I'm going to do the same." He was even cuter than his friend.

"What a sweet gesture, but I'm married." I tried to hand him back his card.

"It's my business card. I own a rental car company, so if you ever need a car, or you are suddenly single, give me a call." He turned before I could insist on him taking his card back.

Both I and Zee stood in the middle of the restaurant speechless, servers whisking around us on both sides. After I regained a little composure I pulled her along. Once we maneuvered through the people standing near the door, waiting for a seat, and were outside, I looked around to make sure they were gone, or at least not standing within earshot.

"Do you plan on breathing?"

"I'm trying. Can you believe what just happened to me? Never has anyone come on to me that way. He was way too cool. And I look like this." She waved her hand up and down her body.

"You are beautiful, and that's what he saw."

I couldn't understand why she was obsessed with her weight now. She was concerned before but never this concerned.

"Well, I'm going to call him," she said, tucking the card away in her purse, "but not until I've shed some of this weight."

As we walked toward her vehicle, I said, "If he approached you today, then I'm sure he doesn't have a problem with your size."

"Then he will really be turned on by the new and improved Zee." She snapped her fingers. "And, chick, you were given a card too. What do you make of that?"

"I don't know, but I'll never be suddenly single. So he can scratch me off the hit list."

I thought of Jeffrey, who knew I was out shopping, and wondered if he was still playing golf with Blaine. Once upon a time, if I was away from him for longer than a few hours, he'd call and just say he needed to hear me breathe. I used to think it was so silly. How could anyone be comforted by a breathing sound?

When I thought about it, though, I realized I'd lost count of the nights lately that I'd softly put my head on his pillow, closed my eyes, and just listened to him breathe. It reminded me that, although I felt he was drifting away from me, he was still there.

I'd lay there in the silence of the night and breathe in unison with him until sleep overtook me, and then I'd dream life was the way it used to be, when we were good and everything was connected in all the right places. In his arms I would feel so at ease, knowing, in the seconds between those moments, right when I could feel the bliss of our connection, he'd kiss me.

I wasn't sure why things were different, or why he chose not to talk to me or acknowledge that things were slightly out of harmony, but he was still my husband and I was still his wife, for better or for worse.

Chapter 13

Cassandra

Gabby walked behind me talking a mile a minute. She had long ago given me a headache and was plunking my last nerve. I was two New York minutes from snapping on her. That's how I knew we were right back to normal. The novelty of my return was wearing off, and I felt so back at home, all the awkwardness was long gone.

"I don't know why you're so upset, and I know you can't be scared to do this. It's a play. It's hanging out with a family friend. A few days ago, you were all giggles."

"I'm not scared—Get it straight from the gate please. I'm just not going. The arrangement was for me and Aunt Debbie." I continued down the hall with the laundry basket. Saturday morning was my designated laundry day, and I was already up and handling the chores of the day. I missed nursing, but this was like private duty with a twist. The added bonus was, I was caring for someone dear to me. I had already lost too much time, so this was sort of like a makeup. How in the world could I complain? I wasn't scared to hang out with the man. Without Aunt Debbie there for physical interference, I would have likely made another fool of myself, and if there had been any doubt that I was a little attracted to him, it would have been confirmed, since I wasn't good at hiding my feelings. This was enough to deal with, but I was determined to tell Gabby and Aunt Debbie about the invisible marriage sooner than later.

Gabby pulled the sheets off the bed while I gathered a few other things from Aunt Debbie's room. "Well, I know she wanted to go. I don't think she prayed for gout." She laughed. "Who would want their big toe to swell up the size of a plum?"

"Girl, you need to stop laughing. That stuff is painful. She didn't even want me to cover her foot up. You should have seen her face when I accidentally placed a pillow on it. Talking about grunting, I think she was grunting in tongues."

We both laughed until tears came out of our eyes.

Gabby was laughing so hard, she held her sides. "You going to hell for that one."

"And you will be holding the door, Ms. Saint." I stood up and finished putting the clothes in the basket. "Well, I left Blaine a message to tell him about Aunt Debbie, and if he wanted just the two of us to go, I think he would have called me back."

I had left that part out when I'd talked to Gabby last night. Right before dinner last night, I had left Blaine a voice mail, and there had been no reply from him. I stayed up until close to eleven, and even when I finally went to bed, I took the cordless phone in with me. To say I was disappointed to not receive a phone call would be an understatement. In a technological world where phone access was everywhere, I couldn't think of anywhere he could be that would prevent him from making a call. But, hey, he wasn't my man. I couldn't even say he was my friend. The brother was just someone I knew.

"Oh. Why didn't you say something earlier about him not calling you? They all went to an overnight retreat, and they won't be communicating until, let's see"—She looked at her watch—"an hour from now. It's something they do periodically, sort of going on a whim without plan or preparation.

Jeffrey doesn't like it, but he follows suit. My husband doesn't want the good church people to see him as indifferent."

While Gabby was going on and on, I was still stuck on the fact that she was just telling me that Blaine had been part of an overnight retreat. "Well, thank you for the tidbit of information, Gabrielle."

"No problem. So now that you know that tidbit of information, you going?

I didn't want to say that I needed to take care of Aunt Debbie anyway. "It wasn't about him not calling."

"Yeah, right. You're lying. But, hey, if you don't want to go to the play, then don't go. Rub Mom's toe, or just look at it from across the room." She took a seat at the kitchen table. "I mean, I could watch the toe."

The rest of what she said was just loud mumbling, nothing really discernible. She was doing it just to irritate me.

Just then the phone rang.

"Hello. . . . Oh, hi. Yes, I'm well, and how are you?"

Gabby leaned back in the chair and just watched me with a smile.

"Hold on please." I pressed the mute button. "I'm a grown woman and don't need you eavesdropping on my conversation. But what you can do, dear sister, is check on Aunt Debbie and Ms. Sadie." I winked at Gabby. "Please."

Aunt Debbie and Ms. Sadie were out on the patio enjoying the sun and listening to a CD of one of the new preachers in the area

"Well, I know when I'm not wanted." Gabby stood up and walked out on the patio.

"I'm sorry. I needed to take care of something. Well, okay, I'll be ready."

It seemed that the date was still on, even without Aunt Debbie. After I heard his voice, it was hard to even form the word *no*.

Gabby came back from the patio and leaned against the refrigerator. "Well, it seems that our evening of theatre and dinner is still on. Should I pick something out for you?"

I had to laugh at the child. It was obvious she was going through a storm in her marriage, and even though she wasn't ready to talk about it, I could see daily that it was bothering her more and more. There was definitely tension between her and Jeffrey. He tried to act all sugary and nice when he came over to the house, but when he thought no one was listening or watching, he didn't play the game of the adoring husband. If Gabby didn't talk to me soon, I was planning on talking to Jeffrey myself. I'd allowed some of my old ways to creep back in because the old Cassie would ask, inform, and dare all in one breath.

"I can pick out my own clothes."

"Well, at least allow me to finish preparing lunch. That's the least I can do. You know I haven't been sharing the load around here like I should, so I owe you the remainder of today, this evening, and some other days."

I looked away and then back at her. "We aren't even close to even. I owe you twenty years."

"No such thing. Now go and pick out something." Gabby finished cutting the tomatoes to place on the plates with the tuna salad.

"What about Jeffrey? Don't you need to spend the evening with him?"

"I asked him to come over and keep me company, but he said he was tired from the guys' shut-in." A sad look came and replaced the happy look she had minutes before. "So all is well on my end."

"Okay, well, why don't we do lunch together and then you can help me find something to wear."

The lights dimmed, and two of the cast of characters came on stage. I watched Blaine out of the corner of my eye and was careful that he didn't catch me glancing at him. His detailed Italian cut navy suit had to be custom-made, the way it hugged his body, and the tie was a perfect complement to the suit, not to mention the French cuff shirt. All of this paled when I was confined in the car with him and took a deep breath. The smell of him intoxicated me.

Blaine leaned over and touched my knee. "Are you okay?"

I jumped. "Oh, yes. I'm fine." I tried to smile.

His touch unnerved me, and I was about ready to run, screaming, out of the theatre, not out of fear but pure panic. The man was getting under my skin. No one had come this close to me since Marco. I'd dated a few guys, but they didn't get behind my tough exterior wall. I didn't know what the heck was happening to me. I could attribute it to lust and being extremely horny. I had no plan of doing him; I hadn't done anybody since Marco, but Marco. So was it lust?

"This is a wonderful play. I'm so glad we came." He turned slightly in the high-back padded seat. "I can't believe that Drake. He is a real character. Can you imagine anyone treating their spouse that way?"

"Oh, no, I can't," I said weakly, having missed all of scene one and scene two.

"I believe that a woman should be cherished and held in esteem. Call me old-fashioned, but a woman has a worth that no man can really afford. And when she gives of herself, it should be truly treasured."

"That's so true. I wish more men thought the way you do. There would likely be less divorces and more marriages."

"I notice you don't wear a ring."

"What?" I looked at him as if he was speaking a foreign language.

"A wedding ring." He spoke slightly louder and pointed toward my left hand. "You don't wear one."

"Actually, I lost my ring right before I left Oakland. We both decided that we'd pick out another when I return." I looked away, hoping he didn't notice how nervous I had become. It was so true about lying. When you tell one, you have to tell another, and before long, they begin to spiral out of control.

"I see." He didn't sound as if he believed me.

"Will you excuse me? I'm going to slip to the restroom before the next scene starts." Before he could respond, I was standing up and on my way to the lobby of the theatre.

Once I was in the ladies room, I didn't bother to go all the way in, but sat down in the outer sitting area and took a deep breath. Nicely dressed women came in and out talking loudly about the play and plans after. When I got myself together, I stood in front of the mirror and pulled my purse open to touch up my makeup.

Gabby had helped me pick out an elegant black, fitted cold shoulder dress with a beaded neckline that draped slightly in the back. There was no need for hose, and I accented my dress with silver Vera Wang diamond-studded ankle-wrap sandals. I topped off my outfit with a single diamond teardrop necklace, with matching teardrop earrings.

When I came down the stairs, Blaine's mouth fell open, and he was speechless, just like I was the last time I'd seen him.

Then he said, "You clean up nice."

Everyone in the room chuckled when Aunt Debbie grunted and nodded her head.

"I think that's her."

I didn't turn around but looked in the mirror at two women who had just come into the restroom. They stood at the other mirror across the room, but I could see they were looking at me. The shorter lady was dressed in a typical beaded dress and some throwback shoes, while the slim lady was put together better and had weave hanging down her back. Not a good look.

"I wonder where he met her at. Have you seen her before?"

Their conversation was hushed, but I could hear every word they were saying, and although they seemed occupied with their own grooming needs, they were totally consumed with me.

"I don't know," the shorter lady said. "I've never seen her before."

They really didn't know me, because if they did, they would know that I was about to introduce myself. I put my lipstick case back in my purse and turned around. "Hello, ladies. I couldn't help but overhear your inquiring questions and I thought I'd introduce myself. My name is Cassandra Price, and I happen to be in the company of Blaine Warner tonight. You were talking about me?"

Neither one of them said anything.

"Well, I didn't want you to be puzzled. Now, as for the rest of the details, the when, the why, and the how, you will have to get those details from him. And if Blaine chooses to share that, then you will know all you need to know." I started toward the door in a cat-like strut, not that it was in my character, but it was totally for their benefit. Just as I was about to reach to open the door, I pivoted back around. "And, ladies, do enjoy the rest of the play and your evening. I plan to."

The lights blinked twice, alerting all of the theatre guests that the second half of the play was about to begin. Everyone increased speed and hustled toward their sections. I merged in with those entering the south wing. When I finally got back to my seat, Blaine stood up and extended a hand to guide me to my seat. A slight jolt went through my hand and I started to pull it back, but instead I swallowed real hard and tried to ignore the sudden feeling.

"Cassandra, it took a while to get back. I thought I was going to have to come look for you." It was a demanding-your-presence tone that sounded full of concern, and his look matched the words that he had just spoken.

"I'm sorry. I was all ready to come back, when I bumped into a couple of your friends." I looked around the theatre and saw them a few rows over. "Oh, there they are." I pointed them out to Blaine. "They were chitchatting with each other in the ladies' room, wondering who I was and how I happened to be here with you."

"What?" He narrowed his brow.

"No worries. I took care of the first part and told them that if they wanted to know the rest, they should ask you." I smiled at Blaine and tilted my head in their direction and waved.

"They are the two nosiest members at Mount Calvary, and they've been that way since the day I stepped foot in the church. Right after my wife died, they baked every dessert under the sun, made chicken and dumplings and every other enticing country entrée every other Sunday. They offered to clean my house, wash my car, walk my dog, take out the cat, not to mention the offer of healing me sexually." He threw his hands in the air. "I'm telling you the truth, you name it, the ladies of Mount Calvary and every other church on the shore offered it. They along with many others that weren't even in the church tried just about everything to get my attention, and Sandy wasn't even cold in her grave."

I listened attentively as he told the story. The mention of

his wife and seeing the light in his eye dim a little caused the moment to turn a little melancholy. "Sandy, that was your wife's name?"

"Actually, it was Sandra, but everyone called her Sandy. She was a wonderful lady. Real sweet, beautiful, and bright. Sandy was full of life and lived life to the fullest. Some considered her reckless because she did things her way and didn't conform to a standard. That was one of the things I loved about her."

The last few words sort of drifted away, and I waited patiently, quietly until the dimness was gone and a little of the light returned.

"It sounds as if the two of you had a very special relationship. I envy that." The words were out before I thought about what I was saying. Sure, it was true, but it likely sounded like I had no special relationship and because I didn't, I likely felt like I was missing out. "I mean, that special oneness doesn't exist in every relationship." I stumbled over the words. "I mean soul mates."

Blaine smiled. "I know what you mean. Would you like to see a photo of Sandy?"

I didn't think it was morbid looking at the photo of a dead person. He must've known I was curious. "Sure."

The word all but popped out of my mouth. Every woman always wants to see the other woman, even if the other woman was no longer on this side. Blaine was just someone I was hanging out with. I had been telling myself that for days, every time he called, every time he came around.

He lifted his body slightly and pulled out his wallet. He opened it up and handing the entire wallet to me showed me a colored photo of a very beautiful golden brown sister. Her eyes were so piercing, and her cheeks held the deepest dimples. Her hair was cut short, and she particularly glowed. In less than a minute, I took in every detail, down to the indigo blouse she was wearing, the diamond tennis bracelet, diamond pendant, what looked like at least half-carat diamond-studded earrings, and the left hand that held on to her right shoulder, creating a stunning poise, sported at least a 2.5-ct. diamond set in a platinum wonder. What he hadn't mentioned was, she was a well-maintained lady.

Of course, I had heard Jeffrey say that Blaine had more money than he could ever spend, and if the man had any worries, money wasn't one of them. And while I hadn't been to his house, again being the curious woman I was, I drove by real slow just to get a look. It was nestled back off the road and the two brick entryway markers held lights that marked the paved driveway. The house itself was something that one would see on MTV cribs. I was so stunned. I went to the corner, turned around, and drove by again real slow. Before I knew it, I had done a ghetto drive-and-look about four times before heading back to Aunt Debbie's.

"Blaine, she is beautiful." I looked at him and hoped that he could see the sincerity in me admiring his wife's beauty. I closed and handed the wallet back to him.

"Thank you. Wait until you see Olivia. She looks exactly like her mom, and so does Zaira, my six-month-old granddaughter. There is already a strong resemblance." He held the wallet another few seconds before putting it back where it belonged. "Listen to me going on and on. Can you tell I'm a proud father and grandfather?"

I smiled. "I can tell you were a proud husband," I said, using my fingers to count off my points. "And I can tell you're a proud father." I was on finger number three. "And I can tell you're a proud grandfather."

He held out his hand and began to use his fingers to count. "Thank you. Thank you. Thank you."

We both laughed.

"So none of those women struck your fancy?" I was curious

now and really wondering, with all the qualities that I had just seen in his wife's photo, what type of woman would come in as a strong number two candidate.

"None of them even came close to making my heart skip a beat or warranted a second glance." He leaned in toward me and looked me directly in my eyes. "It takes a very unique, confident, beautiful, sexy, assertive, and laid-back at times, put you in your place lady, not afraid to be herself, who can handle her business in the kitchen and possesses a passion that's absolutely breathtaking. That's the type of woman that gains my attention."

My mouth was suddenly extremely dry, so much so it caused my throat to get a tickle. I put my hand to my mouth and cleared my throat and coughed a few times. I tried to talk, but nothing came out. I put one finger up to let him know I'd be straight in a minute. Heck, I was thinking, *Man, you've left me speechless. And I think my underwear just might be wet.* "I see. So you haven't found anyone like that yet?"

"I didn't say that. I said it definitely wasn't any of them." Again, he looked directly at me. "What's even funnier is that many of them are friends, and none of them cared which one of them wore me down, so long as one of them did. But then, like now, I'm not interested." He chuckled. "I can't believe you put thing one and thing two in their place. You are a mess. As far as questioning me about the company I keep, they aren't that bold." He smiled sheepishly.

"You never know. There are some bold ladies these days. You are an endangered species, let's face it. There just aren't that many good men left out here. And sometimes the hunter will do just about anything to catch their prey. I'd get a bodyguard if I were you."

"Will you be my bodyguard? I'd like to solicit your services." He smiled.

The lights blinked three times, signaling that things were starting up again.

"I have an idea."

"And what's that, Mr. Warner?" His name just rolled out of my mouth so easily.

"Why don't we give those two something to look at?" Blaine glanced to make sure they were looking.

When he was sure all four eyes were looking at us, he wrapped his left arm around me and kissed me softly on the lips. It wasn't a deep, demanding, yearning kiss, but our lips simply touched together and then parted.

Without thinking of my make-pretend status, and knowing this was all a part of our private show for the two nosy ones, I leaned my head on his shoulder as the lights went down.

Aside from loving a man that didn't love me, and losing a major part of my life believing that one day he would, I dreamed of a different love, and now more than ever, I still did. Somewhere deep down, behind the wall I had erected so many years ago, a little spark ignited. The flame wasn't much of a bright spot, just a glimmer, but it was different from anything else I'd felt. And that feeling settled within my being with simplistic hope.

SUMMER

When the music changes, so does the dance.
—African Proverb

Chapter 14

Gabrielle

"Mrs. Easton, I called because Alexis is an honor student, and she has never been in in-school suspension before. We really thought that would get her back on the right track."

Principal Dennis was sitting before his desk talking about someone who was obviously not my child. Nothing he had said since I walked in came anywhere close to describing the Alexis I'd carried for seven months, raised from the time she breathed her first breath of air, and who was sitting outside this office like she hadn't done a thing and didn't have one care in the world. She had the nerve to greet me like I was there for an awards program.

"Wait a minute, Mr. Dennis. I had no idea Alexis was in in-school suspension for five days. When was this?"

He looked at me like I was a bad parent and flipped his folder open. "All of last week. We sent a note home with her, and the guidance office should have automatically e-mailed you. That's something we started. And if those two measures slip through the cracks somehow, we mail a certified letter." He closed the folder and leaned back, positioning his hands like a steeple.

"Well, this may be a first, Mr. Dennis, but all three of your measures failed. Maybe you had an incorrect address, or your secretary never mailed the letter. I don't know. What I do know is that neither I nor my husband received anything." I was steaming, yet trying to stay composed.

"I see. And where is your husband?"

"He's at work. I didn't bother him because I assumed it would only take one of us to come down here and have this conversation with you."

It was none of his business where my husband was. He was acting like he was building a case against us for not being good parents. I know he should have been able to see smoke coming from my ears.

"Well, I'm not sure where the communication break is. I'm not that familiar with your child, since this is my first academic year here, but she is acting out. As I've said, she is an honor student, and this is all very different. If everything is okay in the home, may I suggesting counseling," he said, practically looking down his nose.

I stood up and placed my purse over my shoulder. "Obviously, Mr. Dennis, what your folder doesn't show is that I am a counselor. A very good one at that." I huffed. "Now, if my daughter needs a professional talk, then I, or one of my very qualified colleagues, would take care of it. Now, I'm going to talk to my daughter and see what is going on. But what you aren't going to do, Mr. Dennis, is paint a picture here assuming that there is a problem at home or anything that would hinder Alexis from sharing, other than the typical sixteen-year-old who just doesn't want to tell her mother and father, 'I'm in trouble.'"

"Well, your dau—"

"You do get those cases sometimes, Mr. Dennis, don't you? I mean, there were times when I, a top, honored graduate from a real accredited school of higher academia, didn't always share things with my parents when I felt it would be to my disadvantage to do so."

"I understand your point, Mrs. Easton." He was beet-red. "I had no idea you were a counselor." He flipped through the folder. "I mean, it's not in this folder anywhere."

"As I said, I will talk to my daughter, and please be assured that I will deal with all of this. Have a good day." I walked out of his office and glanced in Alexis' direction. The look on her face changed the minute she saw the look on mine. I didn't say anything to her as she followed behind me.

Once we were in my truck. I put my key in the ignition and started the vehicle, turning the air up on high. I seriously needed to cool off. Without looking in her direction, I asked, "What do you have to say?"

"How was your day?"

"Young lady, this is not funny. On second thought, don't talk to me. Don't exhale or inhale all the way home. I don't even want to know that you're in the car."

I talked under my breath all the way to the house, using my hands to talk to myself. This child was trying to drive me crazy.

Alexis didn't speak all the way home but looked out the window. She jumped out of the car as soon as I pulled into the driveway and used the key to open the front door, turning off the alarm once she was inside.

I caught up with her just as she was getting a snack and something to drink from the refrigerator. "Give me your cell phone." I put my bag down and my purse on the arm of the chair.

"What?" she said, her voice high-pitched.

"Alexis, don't play with me, and please don't disrespect me. Give me your phone."

She reached in her backpack and handed me the phone, big crocodile tears welling in her eyes. "May I go to my room?"

"You sure can." I wasn't moved by her tears. They didn't happen until I'd asked for her phone.

Just then Jay came through the door. "Hey, good looking. What you got cooking?" He threw his backpack on one of the chairs and kissed me on the cheek.

"Hey, Jay. How was your day?" I stood up and walked to the freezer, trying to figure out what I could thaw in time for dinner. I definitely didn't feel like going back out to the grocery store.

"My day was good. But, seriously, what you got cooking?" He lifted his head up and sniffed the air.

"Nothing yet," I said, continuing my search.

"You were just at school?" He popped the top on the juice and drank all of it in almost two gulps.

"Yes, I was." I waited to see what he was going to say.

"Yeah. Brooks said he saw you and Alexis coming out of the office." He sat down at the kitchen and waited, like he had something to say.

"What's up, Jay? What's going on with your sister? And why didn't you tell me she was in in-school suspension?"

"Mom, we've had a pact forever. Neither tells on the other, and neither comes home and shares anything, unless it may cause the other hurt, harm, or danger." He looked at me.

"Okay, I understand that, and I even respect that. Is there anything I should know then?" I closed the door to the freezer and took a seat across from him.

"Alexis been hanging out with Seed." Jay started beating on the edge of the table.

I was about ready to snatch him. All this one-sentence stuff, when I was waiting for all the information. I reached over and hit his hands.

"Oh, I'm sorry, Mom. My bad."

"Who the heck is Seed?"

"His name is Simon, but we all call him Seed. Because he's a bad seed."

He was about ready to leave it at that, until he saw me narrow one eyebrow. "He's bad news, Mom. He sells drugs, and some say he uses them too. Alexis started hanging out with him a few weeks ago. I told her, if she continued, I was going to tell you and Dad. So I have." Like a secret informant, he was up from the table and gone.

I sat there for a few minutes, unable to move. I wasn't trying to let history repeat itself. Cassie had been swayed by the same type of guy, and while everyone else saw and knew what Marco was about, she didn't. It was very likely that Alexis didn't see it either.

I put on my counseling cap and began to come up with solutions and strategies to help her see reason. I'd have to tell Jeffrey, but before I did, I needed to digest it myself. And right now it wasn't going down well. I'd share it all with Cassie and pray that she could help reach her. I'd even ask Mom to use her one good hand and rub her down with some blessed oil.

Dr. Johns stood in the doorway of my office. "Hey, I'd like to see you about your client list. I have two group sessions I want you to put together."

"Oh, sure. Just let me know when you want to talk." I rubbed my neck a few times and tilted my head. It was absolutely busting with a headache.

"What's wrong?" Dr. Johns walked into my office, placed the two binders on a nearby table and closed the door.

"I haven't been sleeping well."

I got up from my chair and sat on the windowsill, hoping some sunrays would warm my body.

I had been thinking about what had happened last night. Jeffrey came home early, and after we talked about Alexis for hours, we showered apart, of course. He did manage to lay across the bed with me, and we continued chatting. He even let me lay in his arms.

Things were going in the right direction, and I was so hopeful. It felt good just being that close to him without being pushed away or thrown across the room for being that close. The room was dark, but the lighting from the television in the distance cast enough light that I could see his face.

"That feels so good." I mumbled. I slipped the chemise I was wearing over my head and moved my body on top of him. I kissed him on the neck and rubbed my hands over his shoulders and down his chest, watching his expression the entire time.

After a few minutes, I leaned down to kiss him, and he turned his head slightly. *Okay*, I thought. I slipped my hand in his lounge pants, and there was no reaction.

"I'm not in the mood, Gabrielle. Let's just go to sleep."

I tried to look in his eyes, the eyes that held the look of desire that said he wanted me but he had turned away. What did I see then?

I moved my body off him and slipped my gown back on. I sat on the side of the bed for a while in silence then got up. "I'm going downstairs for a while to read." I waited for a reply. When none came, I added, "I love you."

"I love you too," he said, his voice muffled.

I walked out and closed the door behind me. On the other side of the door, I looked around. I didn't know what was going on. My husband went from not kissing me, to not wanting to make love to me. Down the hall was my daughter who was dating a thug. I was a counselor and every day, new events and circumstances in my personal life were proving that I needed help. Some likely thought I had it all together, but my inner circle knew better, and each of them, Cassie, Zee, and Mom was waiting for me to open up. I thought of something I'd heard in a class years ago—If a tree falls in the forest and no one hears it, did it really fall?

"It's been very clear for a while, Gabby, that there is something going on with you . . . not because your work is slipping.
And, believe you me, you can't tell by the glory reports I get
from your clients." Dr. Johns smiled. "I'm a trained professional as well. I can tell that there's something heavy wearing
down on you. I don't have to tell you that if you're not careful it will eat away at you or end up costing you more than
this free session I'm about to offer you." She came over and
touched my shoulder.

Before I knew it, I had unleashed the entire ordeal, and
even though I cried my way through it all, I didn't leave anything out. I was about to see just how good a counselor my
boss was.

"I believe you are challenged by this situation because you
don't know whether to react as a counselor or as a wife." Dr.
Johns handed me a tissue from my credenza. "You can't be a
counselor in this . . . as good as you are at helping others. The
emotional attachment is much too strong to put aside. So, the
first thing we will do is assign roles. You, Gabrielle Easton,
will be a client, starting tomorrow at eight A.M., and I will be
your counselor." She walked around the desk and rubbed my
shoulder as I cried silently. "And to further separate roles, as
for today, you are a friend who is hurting, and I'm not here
as your boss, but as a friend who cares about the friend that
is hurting.

"Gabrielle, our premise has always been to seek God in all
that we do. That's why you've been able to do your job so well.
You put Him first and seek Him when it's time to construct a
plan of action. I didn't just drop by today to talk to you about
business. I believe I was sent here because you need me."

I cried even more as my friend spoke.

"You will get through this. You are not alone in this situation. Others have gone before you with similar and sometimes
worse situations. I'm not different. But once I took my profes-

sional hat off and put on the hat of a wife, I was able to slowly put the pieces back together. And once we were fixed by a friend who was my mentor, we were careful not to break the delicate bond that held us together. Many times it's weak with the stresses and worries of this world, the challenge to head households, run corporations, supervise people, be fathers and husbands, and it gets so stretched out, it takes healing, love, and understanding for it to return to some semblance of what could be considered normal."

I was blown away by what she was saying, how on point it all was. I nodded my head, still not able to reply to anything she was saying.

I managed to pull myself together after Dr. Johns left and was busy cleaning off my desk. The conversation made me feel optimistic, but I still had a terrible headache.

Someone knocked.

"Come in."

Zee walked in. "You got a minute?"

"If it's just a minute and if it's not going to cause me to blink in confusion, or push me to think." I kept pulling together the things I would need for tomorrow morning.

"There is something I need to tell you about Cassie. Some things you don't know." She sat down in the chair at the desk.

"And I don't want to know. If there is something you've managed to dig up or think you know about Cassie, you need to discard it. Zee, I'm not interested in second hand. If she wants us to know something, then she will be the one to tell us. I know there are some things that she needs to share, and in her time she, will, not your time." I sighed.

Zee sucked her teeth. "I can't believe you don't want to know what she was up to before she came back home."

"I don't care, Zee. Now, please go on back to your office. I'm going home." I placed my purse on my arm. "I love you enough to tell you to leave it alone. What is going on will come to light, or it won't." There was no reason for me, or anyone else for that matter, to judge.

I had so much to think about. Dr. Johns had definitely opened up plenty to think about in what I guess I would consider her first session.

Chapter 15

Cassandra

"Aunt Debbie, I'm so proud of you." I reached down and hugged her tight. While she had trouble lifting up her right hand, she attempted to try to lift up the good hand and pat my back. "The therapist said you are making great progress and your sounds are beginning to separate and pretty soon they will come together and form a few syllables, and before long, you'll be speaking words, young lady."

"Yeea." She nodded her head up and down slowly.

She was doing well, and we were all so proud of her. Everyone, including Blaine. After the play, we had been hanging out frequently, and almost every other night he was over playing bingo, having dinner, or just watching television. I was coming up on my third month at home, and he had slowly become a constant. I think he'd known all the time that my marriage wasn't that happy. And still he was the perfect gentleman, never coming on to me at all. Sure, he would say things that could be viewed as an expression of interest, and would compliment me, and occasionally give me flowers or chocolate. But he never overstepped those boundaries.

A few days after the play, he invited me and Aunt Debbie for dinner at his house, and I jumped at the chance. This time I'd get a chance to actually get inside the mansion and not just drive by. I laughed every time I thought of how ridiculous I must have looked.

The visit was wonderful, the meal so tasteful, and his company, I just couldn't put that in words. I'd met both of his kids, their spouses, and the grandkids. For some reason I felt like I was being inspected, the way they looked me up and down, and asked me all kinds of questions about everything except being married.

I flipped through the *Essence* magazine, taking in the latest hairstyles and clothing lines for the fall. It was time for me to do something with my hair. Me and Gabby both said we would do something bold and daring for the fall. We just didn't know what.

Aunt Debbie was on the sofa taking a nap with her favorite throw blanket over her legs. It was ninety degrees outside, and she would point to let me know she was cold. Then she would make a bunch of noises that together meant, give me something to cover up my legs and turn the air down or off. It was usually so warm, you could cook without having to use the range.

There was a knock on the door and I glanced at the grandfather clock in the corner. It was too early to be Blaine, and I knew that Gabby had back-to-back appointments today. Jeffrey only came in the evening, and we weren't expecting anyone. But then it could always be someone from the church.

I put the magazine down and pulled my shirt over my black tights. After the busted, tore-up sweatpants episode months ago, I held to my promise. My daily attire was always presentable. I had picked up a few pounds, but was far from where I used to be. I was making regular visits to the gym on my two available mornings, and was walking Aunt Debbie in her wheelchair around the yard almost every day. I was in good shape and felt super.

I paused in front of the mirror to make sure my hair was okay. Pleased with what I saw looking back at me, I went to answer the door. Comfortable in my country home, I opened the door without pulling the curtain back.

"Hello, sweetheart." Marco was standing there grinning from ear to ear, looking fresh as always in his usual summer attire, sneakers, jeans, and some type of polo shirt. He smelled good too.

"What are you doing here?" I stood in the doorway looking at him, wishing I could blink like Jeannie and he'd go away.

"Is that any way to talk to your one and only. Can I at least come home?" He looked so innocent, which he never was.

This time seeing him was nothing like our last encounter at the airport. I was no longer attracted to him, and the stronghold he had on me and my heart was no longer there. I wanted to run down to the church and get on my knees and thank God.

"You can, but you will not be staying long." I turned my back, and he came in and closed the door behind him.

"The house looks different."

"It's been a long time, Marco." I sat down at the kitchen table.

"That it has." He sat down in the chair closest to me. "Aren't you going to offer me some tea or lemonade, Southern-style?"

"As I said, you will not be staying long." I remained seated, my arms folded, my elbows on the table.

"Excuse me. Well, it looks like you aren't coming back to Oakland. I mean, you sublet our place to your friend, you were laid off at the hospital, which I still can't figure out why you didn't tell me. I would have been more than glad to foot the bills at the condo and take care of you as well. It's not like I can't afford it."

"That wasn't necessary." I continued to look at him, displaying no fear or uncertainty.

"Well, I figured you were relocating, so I, being the good mate, decided to bring some of my business back to Virginia. That way I can handle some business and see you too. What a brilliant plan." He held both arms up in the air and clenched his fists.

"No, it's not a good plan. I want you to go back under the rock you came from. And your business disgusts me, and I never have, and never will, want anything to do with it. I never allowed you to take care of me with any of the money you earned. You loved the game and the business much more than you ever loved me, not to mention the many women. Whatever flavor of the month you had, you never came to me unless you were in-between women, or you came because you'd made me your sexual charity case." I felt tears threatening to fall. I swallowed hard. "I was too weak at one point to see that I was no charity case. Being back home has been good for me. And I want you to get back on a plane and go right back and live life there, not here."

"I can't believe you feel like that. You know I was your big daddy. Always was and always will be. Now, if you talking with all this confidence and newfound freedom, it must be some man you seeing." He leaned back in the chair. "Most times in order for a woman to get over one man, she got to replace him with another man."

"Think whatever you want to think. It's not about another man, it's about me coming to my senses finally. Marco, I did that before I ever left Oakland, and I took the time to tell you that before I left. You just assumed that I was talking outside my neck. But the news is, I was so serious."

Before he could reply, there was another knock. *This had*

better not be the same Jehovah Witness that came last week. Again I swung the door open without looking.

"Hey, beautiful."

"Oh, hello," I said to Blaine. I could have fallen over. *What in the world is going on today?*

Without another word, he came right on in the way he always did. When he saw someone was in the kitchen, he stopped dead in his tracks. "Oh, I didn't know you had company."

Marco stood up. "What's good, man. My name is Marco Brent. I'm Cassandra's significant other," he said, referring to himself the way he always did. He could never say *husband.*

"Hello. I'm Blaine Warner, a friend of the family. Look, Cassandra, I know this is Pastor Taylor's nap time, but just let her know I have that information she wanted me to get." He was already turning back toward the door.

I didn't want to look directly at him, but I didn't want to look away either. There was no way I wanted this to unfold this way. I was planning on telling the man I wasn't married. I wanted more from Blaine and knew he felt that way too, but before I could even position myself as a possible suitor, I had to be honest. He deserved my honesty.

"I'll tell her. Why don't you come by later?"

"I might do that. Well, you take care and enjoy your visit."

After he closed the door behind him, all I could do was close my eyes. There was hurt on his face, and I had put it there.

"So that's him? Old dude is trying to beat my time. He must be taking some serious Viagra, if he rocks you better than me." He stood against the refrigerator looking so cocky.

"It's not like that. We're friends. You should try it some time. It's when you have a female friend that you don't just jump in bed with." I began to wipe the countertop off, even though it wasn't dirty.

"I see you got jokes. Come all the way back to the Eastern

Shore and decide to become a comedian. Ha! Ha! Look, I'm going to leave for now. I got some connects to make, but I'll see you later." Marco walked over to me and leaned down to kiss me.

"Don't you even think about it." I wasn't sure what to do if he went forward with his plan of letting his lips come any-where near my face.

"Later on then. Be sweet and keep it tight." He started laughing and walked out the door.

I wiped the countertop until the anger and the pain over-took me and tears fell. *How could he come and mess everything up?*

I walked in the family room to check on Aunt Debbie. She was wide-awake. "How was your nap?" I wasn't sure how long she had been awake. I wondered if she'd heard me and Marco talking.

She grunted and nodded.

"Aunt Debbie, there is so much I need to tell you . . . so much I want to say. I never told you how sorry I was for leav-ing you. I owed you the world, and I turned my back on you."

The tears from Marco were mixing with the tears I had stored up. I kneeled down in front of her. "Now Marco shows up, and I've fallen in love with Blaine." That part was out before I even realized it. "I'm not married to Marco, Aunt Debbie. He carried me to Oakland and treated me so terribly. I struggled to make it. At times I didn't even have food on my table. But I never took any of his drug money. I would go hungry before I took his dirty money." I wiped my nose and continued. "It was so hard. I worked two and three jobs to get myself through school, but because you taught me to be strong in the face of adversity, I made it. I regret telling you guys I had my own business. I never did. I was a nursing super-visor at one of the biggest hospitals in the area. That should have been enough, but I wanted to impress you. I wanted to come back somebody."

The tears flowed heavier and I couldn't stop them.

"I love Blaine, Aunt Debbie, and Marco has messed up any chance I may have." I laid my head in her lap and cried.

She rubbed my head. I knew she was trying to make me feel that everything would work out, that everything would be just fine, but I didn't feel that way at all.

Chapter 16

Gabrielle

Almost everything in life was worth a second try, so even if there was another woman, I wasn't just going to hand my husband over on a silver platter. In between my patients, I had several sessions with Dr. Johns. It didn't take me long to conclude that a good offense is the best defense, or something like that. I had already endured the hit of rejection, so I wasn't planning on knowingly taking the hit of an extramarital affair from him.

I pulled my cordless phone out of my clinical jacket pocket and speed-dialed my husband's cell phone. I glanced at the clock on my desk. I wanted to catch him before he left for lunch. Just as the phone started to ring, I turned the chair around and looked out the window. The lawn care service was on premises, and the smell of freshly cut grass slipped under my slightly cracked window.

"Hello."

"Hey, sweetie." I tried to sound as sweet as I could. I wasn't feeling it, but I reminded myself of my last session. "I know you're getting ready to go to lunch, but I wanted to see if you mind us going out tonight."

"Tonight?"

I wanted to yell but counted down. I shouldn't have to jump through hoops to get him to be with me. It seemed I was going the extra mile and he wasn't trying to meet me halfway.

"Yes, the kids will be going to something at the center, and then they are hanging out with Mom and Cassie. Remember them talking about it this morning." It was only a few hours ago. He had to remember that.

"Oh, yeah." He was slow to add, "If you want to go out, it's fine with me. I'll be there my regular time."

"Great. Well, I'll see you then." I hung up.

Saying that I loved him at the conclusion of the conversation was my usual ritual, but I had trouble just asking my husband out. I was stressing so much else, I didn't need to stress that too. It wasn't like he was holding the cell phone waiting for those three magical words.

Now, that I knew all systems were go, I picked the phone back up and dialed the receptionist. "Hello, this is Mrs. Easton. Please cancel the rest of my appointments for today."

I left work and pulled Cassie away from Mom, who I knew would be with the speech therapist for a couple of hours. We were browsing the racks at Victoria's Secret.

"Cassie, help me pick out something that screams *seduction*."

"Okay, I'm looking."

We continued to browse in serious silence.

"Oh, look at this." She held up a red silk gown with splits on both sides and a matching thong. "I like this. I think it would look good on me."

I looked at her as if getting ready to throw a dagger. I pointed at my head. "Focus, Cassie, focus."

"Why are you so uptight? You are planning a special night with Jeffrey. That shouldn't be stressful."

"It is, if your husband avoided you like the plague, and if you've only made love three times in months and it had nothing to do with love but seemed like raw sex. And, oh yeah, he won't kiss me. No hello, good-bye, good night, see you later, glad-to-see-you kiss. No kiss at all."

Cassie put the gown back in its place. "I knew something was wrong, and I knew in time you would tell me. Of course, I didn't expect any of this. Do you think . . ." She paused.

"What? That there is someone else? Of course, I do. Then again, I don't think there is. Heck, Cassie, I don't know what to think. But, right now, we are planning a night of seduction."

"Okay. Well, you know you can't let this be your fault. You've been and are a good wife and mother. Don't get caught up in thinking that you've done something somehow. I know you tell women that, and I'm telling you that."

"I know."

Cassie was right. I wasn't sure why I didn't tell her sooner.

After we'd finished shopping and I'd picked out everything I needed, I dropped her off just as Mom was finishing up.

The rest of the preparation time went quickly. Before I could really get myself together emotionally, Jeffrey was coming through the garage door. I was sitting in the family room flipping nervously through a book. I waited to see if he was going to acknowledge my presence.

"Hey, sweetie. Let me feed Sable and shower, and we can leave." He placed his laptop case near the table.

"Already done. Sable is fed, happy, and probably dreaming about now."

"Good. Well, I won't be long." Jeffrey whistled as he went upstairs.

I looked over toward his laptop case and considered checking, to see what I could see. A crazy thought. I had never done anything like that, and regardless of what could be happening, I wasn't dropping down to that level. I dismissed it and waited.

Jeffrey finished dressing in record time, and we were off to the restaurant. Conversation was slow, but didn't seem forced or strained. By the time we got there, we were right on time for our reservation.

"Oh, this is so nice." I looked around the room that was set up just for us and smiled. A glance in Jeffrey's direction and I could tell that he approved.

The table was situated by the window that overlooked the beach, so we could hear the sound of waves against the rocks. The atmosphere was so romantic as we sat near the window and watched the waves. We talked about the kids, work, and a little of everything else as we relaxed and ate lobster tails and stuffed shrimp.

"Okay, on to part two." I rubbed my stomach, almost ready to call it a night at this point. I didn't bank on becoming so full.

"And what is part two, may I ask?" Jeffrey was a lot warmer than he had been in a long time.

"Just walk with me."

We went right out to the boardwalk, and I reached for his hand. "Do you remember the first time we came here together?" I asked.

"I sure do. It was right after we started dating in college, and you brought me home to meet your parents. We came here that evening."

He was absolutely right. I was impressed.

"I was already in love with you." I waited to see what he had to say. "You know I was in love with you from go."

"I know you won't believe this but, Gabrielle, I loved you from the very beginning. And I knew I continued to mess around after we started dating, but it was never anything serious. God, do I wish that I hadn't done any of that. I should have been focusing on being committed to you."

I wasn't sure why he was zeroing in on that. It wasn't in Jeffrey's makeup to be all that apologetic. I worried that he was trying to tell me about some affair he was having.

"Well, we ended up together, and we got through those times, so I say it all worked out."

We walked a little longer.

"Gabby, we should probably head home. It's getting late, girl. We can't hang out all night long like we used to. We aren't exactly spring chickens."

"Speak for yourself." I laughed. "We don't need to worry about going home though. We have a room at the Resort and Inn."

I was pretty proud of myself. In a matter of four to five hours, I had made reservations, did a little shopping, and packed us a bag. Not half-bad, if I say so myself.

"Okay, well let's go." I couldn't read his expression and I didn't want to try too hard for fear that I wouldn't be happy with the way he really felt about the romantic evening I had planned.

We drove the short distance and checked in. The room was absolutely breathtaking, with its ocean view. For a while we stood on the balcony. He wrapped his arms around me, and we stood in silence. There was a tension between us still, and I kept praying we could get past the truth when it finally came out.

"I'm ready to go to bed. What about you?" I looked up at him.

"Yes. It's been a long day." Jeffrey escorted me back to the room.

I lit some candles and took his hand and led him to the bathroom. Very carefully and methodically, I took my husband's clothes off. And he returned the favor. I didn't look down, although I was so tempted. I wanted all of him to come alive with need for me. I wanted, desperately needed to see that.

Turning on the shower, Jeffrey pulled the shower curtain back, and we both got in. We lathered each other down and stood under the blast of hot water. I looked at him as water poured down over our faces. My love for him filled me. I couldn't imagine life without this man.

Hot tears mixed with the water as I looked at him. I could tell that he knew it wasn't just beads of water, but tears. He turned the water off and helped me out. We each dried off and wrapped our bodies in the large fluffy towels.

Making our way to the bed. I couldn't take it anymore. I looked at him all over and I saw need. Without a word, I pushed him on the bed and laid my body next to his as I massaged his chest and kissed around his neck and down his chest. I was trying so hard not to think about someone else touching his body. The tears returned.

Just as I was getting ready to kiss him, he pushed me away.

I started to pound his chest with my fists. "Why are you cheating on me?"

I had to release it all. For months he'd been distant. I knew this could be the end. No matter how much I wanted him and us, if he wanted out, then I couldn't hold him back. It wouldn't be fair to everything we had been to one another.

"I've never cheated on you, Gabrielle. I would never do that to you."

I sat up in bed and wrapped my arms around my knees and didn't dare look at him.

"Listen to me. I love you. There is something wrong with me. That's the reason why I haven't been comfortable making love to you. It's why I haven't kissed you."

My tears stopped just like that. I couldn't believe he was getting ready to hand me some bull. "What are you talking about? What could you have that would prevent you from kissing me? From making love?"

Jeffrey looked down and around, everywhere, but right at me. Then he spoke and it was barely above a whisper, as if someone else was in the room and would tell whatever secret he was about to share. "Gabrielle, this is going to sound crazy, and it doesn't make any sense. I've been to several doctors, and they all said it is possible."

He was scaring me, and I was trying to brace myself for the worst, just in case the worst came. "Just tell me, Jeffrey."

"I have herpes," he said, like it was a sore throat.

That's it. I was numb. He was right. It didn't make sense, unless he had slept with someone, which he'd said over and over minutes ago that he hadn't.

"If you have herpes, how can you sit here and tell me that you haven't slept with anyone else since we've been married? You can only get herpes from sex. I may not be a practicing physician, but I'm on the other side of the spectrum, and that makes no sense." I jumped up and pulled my robe from the chair nearby. "I've given you everything, and you sleep with some ho and risk giving me a disease that I'll have for life." I paced the room, running my finger through my hair.

"Listen to me, Gabby. I swear to God, I haven't been unfaithful. The doctor is saying that I contracted this years ago. It just lay dormant for years, and all of a sudden about five months ago, I had the first flare-up. It can happen." Jeffrey was standing near me, but he didn't come real close.

"I'm not stupid. I know it can happen. I'm just having trouble believing it happened to you." I tried to sit down and popped back up. "If you have herpes, that means I have herpes."

"That is very likely. But, Gabby, it's something we can live with. A few adjustments, and we will be fine, baby." He reached for my arm.

"Don't *baby* me. Now you want to baby me? You haven't so much as helped me across the street or down the steps, and now you talking baby. You've been evasive, nasty and cold and all the time it had nothing to do with me, but everything to do with your dirty trifling behind, laying up catching some nasty-person disease."

"Please, Gabby. I'm telling you the truth." Again he reached for me.

I snatched away. "Let's go." I moved around the room, pulling my clothes together.

"Go where? It's two in the morning." He looked as broken as I felt.

"We are going home. This room is too small for the both of us, and right now I don't want to be near you."

I grabbed what I needed, to dress at least halfway, and slammed myself in the bathroom. Once I was inside with the door locked, I collapsed on the floor and cried my eyes and my heart out. I didn't know what to believe. We had herpes. That was reality. If he had it, there was a ninety-nine percent chance that I had it as well. I didn't want to say I was a carrier, because that would mean that I would be carrying the disease in my body for the rest of my life. And I didn't know much about it.

After a few minutes I stood up again, my legs weak. I placed both hands firmly on the counter in front of me and looked in the mirror. The lighting was so bright, it seemed to magnify all of me. I leaned in closer. The room seemed small as I suddenly seemed large against the brightness of it. I wasn't expecting to see something or anything. What I felt, though, was an entirely different matter.

I was breaking up on the inside, and an honest assessment told me it would take a major change of mind and all the winds that could propel us to another place to reach survival from the rock bottom we had hit. It would take all and then some just to stay in love with Jeffrey.

Chapter 17

Cassandra

I walked around all day pinching myself. With the exception of Marco's impromptu visit, everything had been going so well. My entire life had been an episode of holding my breath and always waiting for the other shoe to fall. I'd lost count of all the times it did, and the times when it didn't, well, those I could count on one hand, and I didn't need to use all my fingers.

The last few times we did family dinner, and even when I joined Gabby and Zee for a salon and massage day, Zee was civil to me. Every time she wasn't looking directly at me, I did a careful examination to see if her horns were still there.

Aunt Debbie had made a stellar recovery, saying words, beginning to put a few together. The therapist was so shocked, especially since Aunt Debbie didn't seem all that interested in talking again. The credit didn't belong to me. Still, there was a surge of pride in knowing that she began to come around after I came on the scene.

Before I knew it, the weekend was here, and this was a free Saturday. I rarely got a weekend pass. Gabby had asked me to drop the kids off, right after I'd dropped Aunt Debbie off for the senior day trip to Sight & Sound Theater. She was buzzing around the house, cleaning, when we got there.

"Hey, chick. Where are you?" I said when Alexis unlocked the back door and we filed in.

"Oh, I'm in the laundry room."

I walked toward her voice. Her head was halfway in the washer tub as she threw clothes in. I stood in silence and watched her pull the clothes out of the hamper and throw them in as if attacking something that had the potential to harm her. Once she had a load, she put in laundry detergent, all-fabric bleach, and filled the automatic fabric softener dispenser. When all that was done, she slammed the lid down.

"Did you set out this morning with a plot to kill your laundry?" I folded my arms and pointed toward the washer.

"Got a lot on my mind, Cassie."

She rushed past me and went to sprinkle Carpet Fresh on the carpet in the family room, living room, and down the hall. When she returned to the kitchen, I was standing against the island, still with folded arms. There was something going on, and I wasn't going to leave without her spilling her guts.

This was Gabby and she was always talking nonstop and didn't keep anything to herself. I had wanted so many times to pull her selfishly into my world and unload all that was going on with me, but there was Zee, struggling with her place in Gabby's life since I was back. That struggle became fear that there would be no room for her. I cared too much for her to do that. And I loved Gabby too much to put her in the middle.

"That may very well be, but you are going to stop, and we are going to talk."

She swung around looking as if she was ready to go off on me for telling her what to do. Then she softened, and her arms fell in a sad kind of retreat. "There is something wrong. Come on, let's take Sable for a walk."

I followed her into the garage. Sable must have sensed the mood, because all she did was wag her tail and look up at us. After she put the leash on the collar, we walked out the back door.

The weather was warming up, and according to the forecast, it was going to get hotter, but for right now it was pleasantly warm. I didn't say anything, I just walked.

We walked so far away, the house was no longer visible. Gabby finally spoke. "You know, we went to the beach last night. We had a nice dinner, the food was delicious, and the ambiance was special. Cassie, we walked along the boardwalk arm in arm under the stars. I couldn't have asked for a better beginning. I thought we could bring a little groove back to our relationship, some spice and pop, by getting a room." She smiled to herself. "I arranged everything. We stood out on the balcony looking out at the ocean, and that was, oh my God, an experience. Then after a shower together and just when we were ready to consummate our evening, Jeffrey tells me that he has been diagnosed with herpes."

My mouth fell open. I closed it quickly, not wanting anything to fly in it. It wasn't HIV or AIDS, and I could sigh for that reason alone, but still she was telling me that he had something that wasn't going to go away. *Dag!* Something else hit me. For him to have herpes, he could only get it one way, and she hadn't said that she gave it to him. That means he cheated.

"Oh, sweetie. What? How?"

"The last one was my question. He swore he hasn't cheated, and that he hasn't been with anyone since we've been married. The doctor told him he could have had it all these years and the symptoms just showed up."

"That is possible." I had to support the truth in what he had shared from the doctor. "I've heard of cases like this. Many carriers don't know they are carriers. There are millions of people walking around with it, and they don't even know it. Not everyone shows signs. That's the sad thing." I sighed.

"Yeah, but he could have done some research and came up with this rationale to cover the affair and to keep me from killing him and the sleazy ho he slept with." She stopped walking when Sable moved to the side of a tree to relieve herself. "I mean, I know he could be telling the truth, Cassie, but he could also be lying."

"You know Jeffrey. You've been with him a minute, so you tell me. Does it seem like he's lying about this?"

"Honestly, Cassie, right now I can't tell. I'm so hurt, angry and pissed. I mean, how can I believe Jeffrey hasn't exactly been loyal our entire relationship. He cheated on me up until we said I do. In fact, all the way up to the night before our wedding. I just thought that once we said I do and made a promise to one another, things would be different and I'd suddenly be enough. This is all too much. I can't even think straight."

"Well, then you deal with your range of emotions, and trust me, if you think they are all over the place right now, the next few days are going to be worse. You will want to beat him up one minute and hold him the next. But the most important thing is that you deal with this head-on and not put your head in the sand.

"You need to call your gynecologist and make an appointment. Have a physical examination and pap, and let them do some blood work. Then, day by day by day, you will deal with this. You won't be rash, and at the same time, you won't give him license to get away with anything. Even if he is telling the truth, blocking you out of his life and acting like he has since at least I've been here is not acceptable." I waited for her to say something. I had peeped her hold card from the time I'd stepped off the plane.

"I'm not even going to ask you how you knew we were having problems. I did everything to cover it up."

"That's just it. This is me. You shouldn't have tried to cover it up. Gabby, I know I've been gone and that I kept you at such a distance, but I still feel you, still sense when things are wrong. That hasn't changed."

"I know. I'm sorry. There is no way I wanted to put out there that my marriage was failing. I needed my marriage to really work, to be different. I'd promised myself that."

"Talking to someone, talking to me at least would have made you human. Gabby, I'm here for you to lean on, whether things stay the same, or even when things change. Life is not meant to stay the same. We were created to survive, even in the midst of those changes."

She wiped away a tear. "Tell me something."

I wrapped my arm around her as we strolled along. "What's that?"

"When did you get so smart? You should be the counselor?" She giggled through a crying hiccup.

"I've always been smart. And you are the counselor, and a good one. It's just hard to examine yourself and give yourself advice."

She lifted her head to the sky. "You can say that again. I thank God for sending you home. Cassie, I've missed you."

I was emotionally drained when I walked in the door. When I left Gabby, she was feeling much better. She was acting as if she had been given a death sentence, even though the medical thing could be handled, and the rest could be dealt with.

Jay walked through the back door as I was fixing a sandwich. "Hey, handsome."

I looked up and noticed he had left the door open. Just as I was about tell him to close the door, in walked Marco."

"Hey, Aunt Cassie. Look who I bumped into at the center, Uncle Marco. He rode over here with him. You should see the cool Jaguar he just bought. That thing is bad."

Jay seemed proud of himself, as if he had located something I wanted.

"Oh, I see." I looked past Jay and directly at Marco, who had the same grin I had spent days trying to erase from our last face-to-face.

"Here, Jay. You look hungry."

He nodded and grabbed the plate with the double-decker cold cut with bacon and the chips.

"There's some orange soda in the fridge." I was shaking all over and trying to hide it. What was Marco thinking, picking my nephew up? Scratch that, why was he around him at all?

"Marco, why don't you show me our new car?" I kept a forced smile on my face until we got outside. We were barely off the step when I started yelling, "What do you think you are doing? I can't believe you. That is my nephew in there, and he doesn't need to be around you, Marco. You are foul. He doesn't even need to know you."

"Imagine my surprise when our nephew told me that he was my nephew. Seems I am married to his aunt. Did I miss our wedding announcement? Not that I object." He held his hands up as if defeated.

"We are nothing to one another. Everyone here thought we had married years ago, you know, like you promised. I just didn't correct that when I got here. Do you know how embarrassed I am to return here, knowing that the person I left with and was so madly in love with made a fool of me, used me, and threw me away?"

"That's not the way it was." He leaned against his new car.

"Oh, it wasn't? Now who's trying to fool who? I was there, remember?" I stormed away from him a short distance then turned around. "I want you out of here. It is over, we are over, and I've moved on. You've only come because you don't like to lose."

For once, he was silent and looked as if some of what I was saying meant something to him.

"Jay doesn't need to be exposed. You should never want that for any young man. What if we had a son, he'd be that age and I'm sure you wouldn't excite about passing the family business on to him. These young men need a real hope with a positive expected end. There were so many days when I didn't know if you were going to make it back home. I lived holding my breath, and because I loved you, I didn't have the heart to let you go." There were tears in my eyes. "Marco, let me go. You have a life, and you are okay with what you do. At the end of the day, I'm sure you're proud of the empire you have erected around you. If you've ever loved me, get in that car and leave." I didn't bother to give him another glance. I breathed deeply and walked away.

As I crossed the yard I remembered the night I left. The man standing behind me had been my refuge, what I ran to. Now I was running in the opposite direction.

Chapter 18

Gabrielle

I drove in silence. Even after a week, I still had a heavy weight on me. I always felt like something hanging around my neck was threatening to tilt me over. As Cassie had suggested, I went to the doctor, and in a few days my results would be back. A few days after Jeffrey had spilled the beans, he accepted a month-long assignment with training sessions for his group in Utah. We had sat down and talked about it. Just that, nothing else. And we'd both agreed that his being away right now would be best for me. For his other trips, I used to be right at the airport, holding his hand until he had to go beyond a certain point. This time, he didn't bother to ask me to carry him. A part of me was relieved, and the other part wanted to be there to say good-bye.

"Mom, you just passed the road to the school." Alexis was busy applying eye shadow in the mirror.

"I wasn't going to say a word," Jay said, leaning in the back-seat playing a game on his game system. "It's not like I want to go to school today anyway."

I made a U-turn. "No such luck, my son. To school you are going." I made my way back to our turn and pulled in the temporary parking space to let them out. "Enjoy your day."

Jay jumped out and looked back with a smile. "You too, Mom."

I looked over at Alexis, thinking she was still putting on

makeup. I was ready to drill her about wearing makeup too early. When I turned, she was just looking at me. "What?"

"Mom, I'm sorry about what happened with Seed. I'm not seeing him anymore, and I know it was all wrong. Aunt Cassie told me all about Uncle Marco and I would never want anything like that to happen to me and I'd never turn my back on my family. She says it was the worst decision she ever made, and I wouldn't want to feel that way." Alexis' eyes began to water. She reached over and hugged me tight.

I held on to her, relieved and moved. "I accept your apology, and I love you."

"Okay." She dapped at her eyes and opened the door and got out.

I rode to work with at least one thing off my mind.

Zee's surgery was postponed to next week since there were a few tests they needed to repeat, so I could give everything else my undivided attention.

I walked through the lobby. This morning, I was determined to be upbeat. I dressed to impress myself, and it did wonders for my mood. "Good Morning." I nodded at the security guard. I was earlier than usual, and the office building was pretty empty so far. Waltzing into my office, I wish I could rewind before Jeffrey's bomb. Still, as Cassie said, it was there and I had to deal with it.

Going over my notes didn't take as long as I thought. I still had an hour before my appointment. What was I going to do? I played with the stress ball, rolling it back and forth. My sessions had been ongoing, and I was equipped to handle this. I was just putting too much pressure on myself. I needed to just relax.

Chapter 19

Cassandra

I was singing all the way up the back steps. Something about sunshine on a cloudy day. This was truly a cloud I was on, and I was enjoying every single, solitary moment of it. I couldn't even imagine what my life was like in sunny California. Life was great right here on the Eastern Shore. It just went to show that happiness was a state of mind, and location, location, location had nothing at all to do with it.

Blaine had picked me up just to hang out. We'd started at the mall and ended up at the outlets, where I did a little shopping and a lot of window-watching.

Blaine and I stood at the jewelry store counter going back and forth.

"Listen, I'm not buying you the watch to entrap you."

"I know. But I can buy my own watch. And I don't have to have one that cost this much. When it comes to a watch, I'm just a plain Timex girl. That way if I should misplace it or something happens, I don't feel so bad." My watch had fallen off the other day and broke while I was playing with Sax, Blaine's very big, very aggressive German shepherd.

"You remind me of Sandy. She would spend an arm and a leg on a purse or shoes that she couldn't wear because of course it doesn't go with everything, but a watch which, mind you, can be worn daily, on that, you select something cheap." He started laughing.

The sales person came back, and when she noticed we had still not had a meeting of minds, she laughed along with us.

"I see your point. I really do." I pushed my overpriced Dooney and Bourke bag on my shoulder. "Aunt Debbie always told me to never let a man buy you a watch—"

"Heard it so many times before. And since I have age and wisdom on you, let me tell you, it isn't true. Time will never run out on what is meant to be, unless it's God's will, and then you will be left with wonderful memories."

I could tell he was talking about Sandy. Mention of her was becoming more and more frequent.

"With that said and our decision made, we will take this watch and I'm actually going to go ahead and place it on her arm." He placed the platinum and diamond dialed watch on my left arm and raised my hand to kiss it.

I cleared my throat and when he completed the task of kissing me there, our eyes locked. "Thank you, but I still think—"

"I've won this round. I'll let you have the next."

We walked out of the store fussing over letting me win.

I chuckled about our day as I walked around the living room. I noticed Zee's car in the driveway. I thought maybe Gabby was with her. Walking into the family room, I was smiling from ear to ear. "Hello, family."

"My, my!" Zee said. "Aren't we too happy."

Aunt Debbie swapped at her like she was a mosquito. She knew the truth. I still hadn't had a chance to bare all to Gabby, not with what she was dealing with. It would come, but the time had to be right.

"You tell her, Aunt Debbie. Girlfriend will not rain on my parade."

"Want to bet? Ma Debbie, excuse us. Cassie and I have a long-overdue conversation we must have."

"Don't worry, Aunt Debbie, we will both be good." I looked at my aunt to let her know that nothing Zee could say would upset me.

"What is it, sweetie?" I asked Zee as I pulled a bag of chips from the cabinet. I opened up the bag and held it out. "Want some?"

"No, thanks." She acted aggravated.

"Suit yourself." I put a couple of chips in my mouth and started to chew. I wasn't really hungry. I just craved the salt. We feasted on all-you-can-eat seafood, so my hunger was completely taken care of.

"So tell me, are you enjoying Deacon Blaine's company?" Zee sat on one of the kitchen stools.

"I am. He's a wonderful man." I smiled just thinking about him.

"And an excellent investigator." She paused and looked at me. "You did know he was an investigator?"

"Of course. His company mainly does security, but he does investigations as well. I know everything." I smiled smugly.

"And so do I, thanks to Blaine." She reached for the bag of chips and took a few out.

"What are you talking about?"

"Let's see. Where to start?" She kept chewing as she talked, looking all around as if searching for something. "I know you never married Marco. I know that he was, well, actually, is one of the largest kingpins in the Oakland area. Let's see, you worked at the hospital as a lead nurse or something on the senior floor and you were laid off. You answered phones, etcetera, etcetera before that, and somehow, bless your heart, you worked your way through school. Got your own place after moving out of the projects. It was hard to cover the mortgage most months. Your girlfriend is subleasing it. Of course, there was no sole ownership of any nursing service. Let's see . . . I leave anything out?" She licked the salt off her fingers. "I don't think so. Blaine did a very thorough job. Oh, I know how little money you have in the bank too. So, once you've exhausted that, I'll be glad to give you a loan. Is Marco back in town so you two can start the family business here?"

The wind felt like it had left my body completely. She had just shared all my business and sitting there saying all of this came from Blaine, who hadn't said a word or indicated in any way that he was privy to my past. Whenever I tried to tell him, he would say that my past was my past, that he wasn't interested. I guess he wasn't; he already knew everything.

"You must be real proud of yourself."

"I wonder how my family would feel about you coming back home with your tail tucked between your legs and lying from day one."

"Ma Debbie already knows, and I was planning to tell Cassie. So if you want to tell her yourself, be my guest. I don't think it's going to matter to her one way or the other. She loves me, and she knows that I love her."

Zee didn't matter to me. She just proved that she wasn't half the friend to me that she pretended to be. And she didn't deserve Gabby's friendship either. What I couldn't get over was Blaine. How could he do this? And if he did this before he befriended me, why didn't he share it? Or was he just going along for the ride to see what else he could learn?

"I'm going to ask you to leave now." I looked at her. If I wasn't in my aunt's house, I'd wipe the floor up with her.

"I don't have to leave. This is my family, and you, my dear, don't belong." She refused to move and sat there all confident.

Just then Aunt Debbie rolled her wheelchair in the room, her face twisted as if something was hurting her. She maneuvered directly in front of Zee.

"Ma Debbie, Cassie hasn't changed one bit. Just here getting what she can get, like she did when she first moved in here. I was Gabby's friend, and then she dropped her home-less butt in here."

Aunt Debbie put up her hand. She had to be hurt and disappointed that Zee was going off like this. "Go!" The one word was clear and loud.

"What?" She looked at Aunt Debbie in disbelief.

She repeated. "Go!"

"I think you heard Aunt Debbie. Just leave, Zee. Some-where along the line, you've become bitter, and I feel sorry for you. I've never hurt you, and I never took Gabby from you. There is room in her life for both of us. You have some seri-ous issues. And this is fair warning—You may continue to be in Gabby's life and even in Aunt Debbie's, but stay away from me." I opened the door for her to exit.

She looked at Aunt Debbie, who put her head down, and then at me. There was no need for anymore words. She had said it all, and it was indeed a mouthful. There was just one person I wanted to confront right now, and that was Deacon Blaine Warner, head of Warner Security and Investigations.

I made a quick call to Ms. Gladys next door and asked her to come over and sit with Aunt Debbie. Gabby needed to know what happened, but not before I talked to Blaine.

The drive into Maryland was much quicker than it should have been. I drove beyond the speed limit, only slowing in places that the cops patrolled heavily. All the way there, Zee's ugly words echoed throughout the car. I thought of a secret much uglier than those Zee had unleashed. What if Blaine knew that secret too? What if he had the ancient key that could tear my entire family apart? I had to believe that he didn't. There was no way that should ever, could ever, come out. Too much could go wrong, and lives would forever be out of balance.

"You've got to keep our secret, Cassie." Uncle Ed held me on his lap rubbing my back. I felt comforted, afraid and scared at the same time. He was there and I could never move freely around without him watching over me. Doing what he thought would make me feel special. How could it? All of it was so ugly. Too ugly to have a label, and if it did, it would be something that no one could ever say or feel good about saying. That had become what I was then. I fought hard not to be the person that was birthed out of that secret.

By the time I got to Blaine's office, my past mixed and mingled with the recent pain of knowing that he'd betrayed me.

I pulled down the mirror and checked my face. It didn't look as bad as I thought. I'd been a waterfall all the way here. It was a wonder I was able to drive at all. Pushing myself to get out of the car, I walked to the building.

I knew Blaine was in, or at least his pickup truck was parked out front.

"Hello. May I see Mr. Warner?" I said to a young girl sitting at the desk.

She picked up the phone, smiling at me. "Mr. Blaine, Ms. Cassandra is here to see you." She hung up the phone.

She had never seen me before, but she didn't bother to ask who I was. I wondered about that. "How do you know my name?" I looked at her carefully.

"Mr. Blaine has a picture of you in his office. I think you guys took it at the park. He told me your name when I picked it up asking who the beautiful lady was." She giggled. She couldn't have been more than twenty years old.

"Well, thank you, but you are beautiful yourself."

We were smiling at each other when Blaine came out of the office positioned right behind the receptionist's desk.

"Hello, there. This is a wonderful surprise. We've hung out

everywhere else, but never here. You must have thought I was going to put you to work." He laughed.

What he said was funny, but I was in no mood to laugh. When I didn't join him, he looked puzzled.

"Come on in." He moved back around the receptionist's desk and allowed me to go in first. "Jessica, hold all my calls, and I don't want any visitors. Mr. Reynolds will come. Just give him the invoice and tell him I'll call him in a couple of hours."

His office was decorated nicely. The colors were simple and tasteful, and everything matched everything else. And the pieces were large and masculine-looking. As I stood in the center of the floor on a large oriental rug, I noticed our photo on the credenza. The frame was a handsome piece, and our photo looked attractive in its frame. I'd never paid any attention to what we looked like together, but as I looked at the photo, I realized we made a cute couple. Or, should I say, would have made.

Before he could say anything or ask me to sit down, I said, "Did Mr. Reynolds hire you to investigate a family member who just came back in town after many, many years?"

"Cassandra, I wanted to tell you."

"Then what stopped you, Blaine? You befriended me, when all along you were hired to investigate me. You just wanted to keep tabs and see what else you could come up with and carry it all back to Zee?"

"Listen, you don't understand. Initially she wanted to make sure that Aunt Debbie and the family would be okay. She did what she did out of concern for them."

"What was I supposed to be, Blaine? Some demon? Some assassin? Someone who came here to hurt, harm, or endanger them." I turned my back on him.

"I knew that wasn't true the minute I met you that first night. From that point I informed Zee that I would not investigate you any further." He looked directly at me. "All the information I gathered for her was done before your plane ever touched down."

"So if she hadn't told me, you would have never said anything?" I was screaming. "You let me fall for you and allowed me to think that you thought that I was married."

"Cassandra, that's why I was so in touch with you. I was in love with you from the word go. Yes, I knew you were available, a single woman, and by the time you were comfortable enough to tell me, I didn't need the words. Sure, it would have made a difference if you were married. I'm a deacon, and I would never knowingly get involved with a married woman." He stepped behind me and tried to touch my shoulders.

I couldn't believe what he was saying. "You're standing there professing faith, talking about being a deacon, when you helped her stand in judgment of me?"

As much as I thought I knew Blaine, I really didn't know him at all. I needed to get out of here, to go somewhere that he wasn't. That was the reason so many people stayed clear of faith and religion. It was easy for others to judge, without checking to see the cracks in their glass houses.

"I knew it seemed like I was judging, but I wasn't. I was doing a job. I was assuring the safety of people that she cared about and that I cared about too."

"So maybe your secular job compromises who you are as a Christian." I quoted the word *Christian* with my fingers. "I mean, you investigate people assuming they are bad or have something going on negative, when sometimes they just don't. Then you go to church with all your glory to God and say you love your brother and your sister."

"I can see how it looks, but, Cassie, I never meant to hurt you, and as I said, once you were here, I ended it all."

"Don't you ever call me Cassie! Only my friends and loved ones can use my nickname. I don't know you, and I don't want to." I turned to leave.

"Cassandra, don't leave. We need to finish talking." He followed me to the door and out of the office.

"It was nice meeting you, Jessica," I said over my shoulder as I was leaving the office. Jessica sat at the desk, her mouth open.

Once I got to the car, I leaned my head on the steering wheel. Marco had abused my heart way too much to trust anyone else, and here I sat all hurt and emotionally injured because I trusted someone else. I was wide open and so starved for friendship, when the table turned a little, I was eagerly seated there, hungry for a plate.

I started the car and decided that I couldn't really cry over spilled milk. I had my family and I was with them. That's what mattered. Gabby needed me to help her through this rough patch, and Aunt Debbie needed me as well. I could move on and look for the ideal locale to start the next phase of my life, but what I needed was right here. Who knew about tomorrow? Or next week? Or even next month? All I knew was, I needed my family, and they needed me. I'd recover from Blaine somehow, and little by little, I'd get over loving him.

Chapter 20

Gabrielle

"Jeffrey comes home tomorrow." I was beaming. My sessions with Dr. Johns had worked miracles.

"That's great," Cassie said. "And how do you feel about that?" She had been through an emotional battle herself, and when she shared everything with me, my heart was so heavy.

"I'm nervous. I missed him, so it will be good to have him back home."

We had talked every night and even did a few conference calls with Dr. Johns.

"What about you? Have you talked to Blaine?" I peeped at her over my sunglasses.

Cassie was likely to lay me out, but I had to ask. I wanted to know, and so did Mom. We were like enquiring minds.

"Have not, and don't want to."

"I see. Well, he asked for you when I saw him at Bible study last night." Again I looked at her over my glasses.

"Good for Deacon Warner. I'm sure he was wearing his deacon cap and not his secular hat. You know he's two different people, right? Sort of like blended with two different personalities. A chameleon of sorts."

"But aren't we all to a degree?" I wasn't necessarily coming to his defense and I didn't want her to think that. Saying it would likely irritate her and I had just learned that being hurt requires a cooling-off period, and she was still in the thick of her anger.

"Yes, we are, and you are right. It will get better. Who knows, maybe by next year this time, I'll be able to say his name. And the year after that, I'll be able to speak to him."

"This is all running pretty deep," I said, as I drove toward our destination.

"Gabby, I was feeling him deep. I didn't want to, but I did." Her gaze went to the window.

We rode a little while longer, exchanging nothing but silence.

"Well, we are here. You going to be okay with doing this?" I asked.

"I'm good. If she wants to see me, then I can suck it up and oblige. I don't want to be the straw that keeps her from making it in, nor do I want her to be the bridge that keeps me from making it over."

"I couldn't believe that Zee had gone to those lengths to come between us. All this time, I never picked up on the fact that she was a few cans short of a six pack."

"You can never tell what's on people's minds."

We continued through the lobby of the hospital and went in search of the south wing elevators. The hospital was newly remodeled and had just recently received a complete facelift.

"Yeah, but I feel like I could have helped her somewhere along the line. She's been our friend forever, and I worked with her all that time. And while I knew she had some unresolved issues, like with her weight and her mother, I had no idea that she had become borderline-obsessed with our friendship."

Cassie started to laugh. "I don't mean to laugh at you, Gabby. You are saying *borderline*. The girl was in the kitchen acting like she was connected to you at the side. Her eyes were rolling back in her head, and she was repeating your name and rocking."

"Stop exaggerating. This must be the unedited version. You never said any of this before." I joined her laughter. We were making light, but we both knew the situation was serious.

We finally got to her room, and without even nodding, we went through the door. Her head was turned to the window and she was hooked up to an IV and other monitors. "Hey, Zee."

She turned and tried to smile, but she must have felt a pain, because she quickly stopped. "Hey, Gabby." She looked past me and saw Cassie. "Hey, Cassie. Thanks for coming."

"Don't mention it." Cassie didn't come stand next to me, but stood off some distance.

"How are you feeling?" I rubbed her head and reached down and kissed her cheek. She was still my friend, and no matter how warped her mind was, we would somehow get beyond this hump in the road too. I was becoming a pro at getting over things.

"I hurt everywhere. They're going to operate again in an hour or so. Something went wrong, and they need to repair it now." She tried to cough, but it caused her so much pain, she twisted up her face. "They say if they don't fix it, I won't make it."

"Oh, sweetie. You will be just fine, you hear me?" I had no idea it was this bad.

They had rearranged her surgery date for a third time, and after the situation with Cassie, she had refused to see me. She wouldn't open the door or take my calls.

"I pray so." She tried to cough again. "Cassie, I'm sorry." She tried to lift her head up.

Cassie saw the struggle and came closer to the bed. "Don't worry about it, Zee. Just concentrate on getting well. All is forgiven."

"Please . . . I need you to forgive me. I was just trying to take care of the family." She started to cry.

"It's okay, Zee. Really, I'm okay." Cassie reached for her hand.

"Don't blame Blaine. He was telling you the truth. After the initial investigation, he told me, 'No more,' and trust me, I begged, and yet he refused. He loves you. I'm not so out of it that I don't wish it was me. That man is the total package."

We shared a three-way laugh.

"But he loves you. I'm not asking that you forget what happened, but you need to forgive him and allow him to be the man that I know you need."

Cassie said, "Zee, you would never understand."

"Better than you know. We both want a man like Gabby has, someone to love us and be there. I don't know where my Mr. Right is, but yours is there for the taking."

A nurse came in. "It's time for you to get ready for your surgery." She excused herself and reached between me and Cassie to turn a few knobs, adjusting the IV.

"I'll think about what you are saying, but right now both of your friends want you to lay back and relax and think positive thoughts, so you can get all this stuff over with and be the diva that you so desperately want to be. It's hard work to look like this." Cassie put her hand on her hips.

"Well, if I make it through all this, I want to look just like you in a few months." Zee's eyes started to close, and she drifted off.

"Child, go in there and let them fix you up. By next summer, all three of us will be on the beach, making all the other female beachgoers envious." I was praying that whatever had gone wrong would be corrected.

Zee was taking a huge risk, and the physicians had told us that. Her high blood pressure and the other problems she had encountered throughout the recent years had compromised her health significantly. She wanted a child, and if that meant taking a huge leap of faith with the surgery, she was willing to take it.

"That's right, diva. Go in there and handle your business." Cassie's eyes were misty. The usual tough girl had become so sensitive lately, tearing up at the drop of a hat. Somewhere along the line we must have traded places.

"You guys going to be here when I wake up?" Zee licked her lips.

I looked at Cassie. The deal was, once Zee opened her heart and shared whatever she had on her mind concerning their situation, I'd take her home and come back later alone. That was our arrangement before we knew about the complications and that she was going back into surgery. There was no other family. We were all Zee had.

"Both your friends will be right here when you wake up," Cassie reassured her.

I knew it took a lot, but she had taken the high road. I wasn't surprised. That was just the kind of person Cassie was. I was so proud of her.

The orderlies came in to get Zee. Right before they wheeled her out, both Cassie and I leaned over the rails and kissed her cheeks. She mumbled something, but what she mumbled didn't matter. What mattered was, we were here, our friendship still existed, and between us there was enough love to cover the blemish of what happened, all the hurt, the pain and the disappointment.

I was up early and on my way to the airport. Jeffrey's flight wasn't due to arrive for two hours. Before the sun even came up, I was out the door. The kids had mentioned the night before that they wanted to go with me, but I discouraged them. They both missed their father and I wanted their reunion to happen, but I wasn't sure how we would be after our separation.

The telephone therapy sessions had brought a lot out, and I was on my way to forgiveness. For that I was willing to work, no matter how hard. Our marriage deserved that. The one thing that worried me was the forgetting. Dr. Johns had said baby steps. I wouldn't worry about forgetting at this moment, I was too wrapped up putting one foot slowly in front of the other. I'd be taking baby steps until I was able to manage the next phase.

Standing on tiptoe I tried to see over the people standing at the gate. This must have been an executive flight, since nicely dressed men and women, more than fifty of them, filed through the gate, all equipped with tote bag, laptop cases, and shoulder carry-ons.

The long wait took a little wind from my sails. I reached down to check my phone. Maybe he left a message letting me know he was catching a later flight. I turned my back away from the crowd and walked a short distance away to try to capture a private moment. I listened to three messages, but none of them was from Jeffrey. The first two didn't matter, and the last was from the kids wanting to know if their father had touched down yet and to have him call as soon as he did.

It seemed I wasn't the only one who'd missed Jeffrey. Neither of them had missed a night of talking to him, whether they were home or not. They had a ten P.M. agreement when he or either of them was away from home. At that time they'd talk, and he would solve whatever problems they had, or just reassure them that he was available to do so.

"Hey there, pretty lady."

I jumped and turned around.

"Jeffrey. I was just checking to see if your plane was late." He looked so good to me, but I was trying not to show how glad I was to see him.

He was smiling and looking me up and down. "You look good, baby."

I was dressed in jeans, stilettos, and a tight, white body shirt. Nothing special, nothing extra, but I did think I looked nice. My hair was freshly done, and I had on a very special fragrance that tantalized my nose, so I knew it was going to do a job on his.

"Thanks."

We chitchatted about his flight and the kids as we got his luggage. Hardly a quiet moment came between us; there was so much to say. I glanced at him whenever I thought he wasn't looking directly at me. That may have been silly, but I just needed to look at him.

We both were relieved to be out on the road. It seemed like we would never leave the airport.

"I missed you, Gabrielle." Jeffrey reached across the console and put his left hand on my leg.

"I missed you too." I played nervously with a lock of hair and begin to rattle on and on.

After about a half-hour, Jeffrey busted out laughing.

"What?"

"You act the way you did during our first few days. You talked just because you were nervous, but you didn't have anything real important to say."

"I beg your pardon. Everything I say is important. And it was especially important then. I was trying to impress you."

"And now?" He rubbed my leg. It didn't feel like a lustful rub but more like a reassuring touch.

"I just want us to get back to where we were." I smiled.

"That's all I want."

The rest of the drive home, we talked, never mentioning the disease at all. But we both knew that it had to come.

By the time we got home, we were consumed with the kids

and fell in the trap of doing what they wanted to do, which, after visiting Mom and Cassie, was dinner and a movie.

It was late when we got back home.

"What a long day." Jeffrey walked out of the shower, water all over his back.

There I was again, looking at him out of the corner of my eye. "It has been." I was flipping through a magazine, trying to read an article. I had slipped on the nightie I had bought for our special night together that had been short-lived.

"I'm glad to be home." He came on my side of the bed and just watched me.

"What's wrong?" I giggled. Why was I feeling like a school-girl all day?

"Nothing. I just want to thank you for giving us a chance." He looked around our room. "I know it was hard to believe me and even harder for you, a counselor, to get help for us. I was telling you the complete, honest truth. I would never hurt you, and the whole time I dealt with the herpes in silence, shutting you out, was because I feared telling you something that seemed so unbelievable. And to know that I passed it on to you."

"But you didn't." I put the book down and reached for his hand. "I don't know how it happened that you didn't. My doctor isn't exactly sure. Then I was told that I could be infected and just not know it." I paused. "The important thing is that we take care of each other, and change a few things."

"I know. Gabrielle, I love you for loving me," he said softly and slowly.

With great passion, my husband, the man I had fallen in love with, had married, and who was my soul mate and the father of my kids, kissed me. With that kiss, we mentally left our bedroom suite, leaving all that was familiar, to capture a little bit of heaven on earth.

Chapter 21

Cassandra

I was watching Pastor Eddie Long on The Word Network. Aunt Debbie and I enjoyed watching him. After all those times of turning the channel just when some television evangelist came on, not a day passed when we weren't tuned in to somebody.

I got past what I was really feeling about church and realized it was the secret I was carrying that made me resent the concept of a loving God, who'd allowed my world to be rocked that way. Time heals, and it had started to heal that scar. I hadn't talked about it to Gabby, and I hadn't said anything to Aunt Debbie, but I knew and was confident that I would.

For two months I hadn't missed a Sunday in church, and although it was hard to see Blaine and know what almost existed, what came to an abrupt end, I could at least speak and wish him a wonderful Sunday at the conclusion of service, if we happened to get that close to one another. Which I tried to avoid like the plague. But there were times when I just couldn't.

For a while, every time someone knocked at the back door, I expected to see him standing there, all tall and handsome, with a smile that seemed tailor-made just for me. However, that visit never came. When I'd said it was over, that I didn't want to see him, he took my words seriously. Don't get me wrong, I was serious because I was so hurt. That hurt, though, had softened to only a dull ache. It just couldn't compare to the ache I felt at missing him. So many days, evenings, and nights, I wondered if I would wake up the next morning and not still feel him, not still want to laugh and enjoy his company. That morning never came. I was hopeful, though, for whatever would make the change easier for me to bear.

I had fallen asleep in the recliner and was startled when someone knocked on the door. I jumped up, thinking it was just a dream. Aunt Debbie was fast asleep.

The knock came again. I looked at the clock. It was almost ten. I had slept through Aunt Debbie's bath and set bedtime. I didn't realize I was that tired.

This time, since it was so late, I asked who was there.

"Blaine."

I blinked and wiped my face with my hand. My dressing ritual had remained the same even though I didn't have anyone to compliment or enjoy my selection of clothing. It didn't matter I did it all just for me.

I opened the door. "Hello, Blaine."

"Hello. I know it's late, but I need to talk to you."

I extended a hand for him to come in. "What's going on?" I pointed for him to take a seat at the table. I didn't know what my face showed, but I was glad to see him.

"How have you been?"

"I'm good. But I doubt if you came over here to ask how I am." I smiled, hoping it didn't sound like a smart remark. I was just anxious for him to get to the point.

"Well, I wanted to tell you this before you find out some other way." He paused before adding, "Marco was killed."

"What? When? How?"

"It obviously happened yesterday. And he was in Richmond. From what I was told, he was the target of a raid. When the police charged in, he opened fire, and they responded with fire and he was shot."

"Oh." That's all I could say. I wasn't blown away with the news, but I was sad. Sad because I used to love him. It didn't have to end that way. He'd wasted his life. "Well, thanks for coming over to tell me."

"Are you going to be okay?"

"I'll be fine. I'm just sad. I can't say that I'm shocked. I knew one day there was a possibility that this kind of news would come."

He stood, and I followed suit.

"Well, if you need anything, or want to talk, you know how to reach me."

"Okay. Thanks."

We walked slowly to the door.

"Well, thanks again." My heart sank because he was leaving and neither of us was going to stop and say, "What about us?" I wanted to say it. I needed to say it.

Just as he touched the doorknob, he turned around. "Cassandra, I miss you. I haven't stopped missing you. I'm so sorry for what happened. I never meant to hurt you. Sweetheart, I love you."

"You what?"

"I love you. Now, you may not ever forgive me, but you will know that I love you. You will know that, since my wife, no other woman has ever touched me. I never met anyone that I wanted to spend my life with. Someone who I could cherish, and who would cherish me. You are that woman, Cassandra, and I'm telling you right now—I need you."

I opened my mouth and only his name came out. "Blaine."

"I know you are still hurt, and I know because I stood in judgment of you, it affected even your faith walk. I'd never want another to stumble because of what I displayed religiously. There is so much I need to apologize for."

"I accept your apology," I said softly.

"What?" He moved toward me.

"I accept your apology, and I'm sorry for not being willing to listen to you. Zee told me that once you met me, you immediately halted any further investigation and even gave her back her money. I was too caught up to come to you."

He smiled and came even closer. He tilted my head and looked me deep in the eyes. "We've wasted time."

"I know." I smiled, feeling like a major weight had been lifted from my chest. The butterflies returned. "Blaine, I love you too."

"Then all we need to do now is seal it with a real kiss."

Before I could say anything, I was in Blaine Warner's arms, and he was kissing me.

FALL

Tell me who you love, and I'll tell you who you are.
—African American Proverb

Chapter 22

Gabrielle

It was Thanksgiving, and everyone I loved and cherished was gathered around the table. It hadn't been a whole year since Cassie had returned home, but what a whirlwind ten months it had been. I never knew so much could happen in such a short period of time.

The day was a long one, but the ending of it, I will never forget. Mom motioned that she wanted to talk, and both Cassie and I followed her to her bedroom. After pulling her wheelchair to the corner of the dresser, she took out a wrinkled, folded letter.

"What's this, Mom?"

She looked back at me. "Read."

As me and Cassie and I sat on the bed and I unfolded the letter, Mom rubbed her hands together.

I breathed hard and started reading:

My dearest girls

I hope that you are reading this and God has given me favor and I am still with you. Whether I am or not, you two must know that I love you both with all my heart and my soul. Gabrielle, you are my angel, and I was blessed with you, even though I was told that I would never have kids. You made a liar out of the devil, and here you are, my special blessing. Our family was not complete, though, and He opened our door and our hearts to Cassandra. I promised Cindy that I would care for her child and treat her like my own and I do. I pray, Cassandra, that you have never regretted being a part of us. But there is something you must know. Life has a way of giving you a challenge and sometime an obstacle that can seem hard to overcome and harder often to live with. I took the challenge and I accepted what came and it has never by grace been hard for me to live with. I'd love Ed from the day he walked into my life and I spent my life trying to be all I could be to him. But no matter how hard I tried, I was never enough.

I swallowed back tears as I looked at Cassie.

They say that you can't control your heart nor who that heart loves. That was true in Ed's case, because although I was his wife, he fell in love with another woman. While I suspected, I never knew, and really a part of me never wanted to know, because it would mean losing him, and I could never bear losing Ed. He was my world.

There were rumors of this woman and that woman, and if it were true, he was with them, but there was still just one woman that he loved. Cassie, when your mother became ill, I wished many days that I could have been given the power to heal her infirmity. But that was not to be. Each day she grew weaker, and when the end drew near, she asked me to accept the very thing that would hurt me more than anything, and make the sacrifice to live with it for the rest of my life. Wanting her to be at peace, I accepted. How could I have prepared myself for the truth? When my blood sister asked me to take care of her child, she was also asking me to care for my husband's daughter.

I dropped the letter on the floor and looked at Mom with empathy and hurt. I was so shocked.

Cassie picked the letter up and continued with tears in her eyes.

I did as she asked and I brought my sister's daughter and my husband's child into our house. And I never uttered a word to him of what I knew to be the truth. It was the secret I shared with my sister. I wanted to hate him, but isn't it funny, the very thing you tell your heart to do doesn't always happen, so I kept right on loving him until the day he died. And until the day he died, he kept right on loving Cindy. In death she still held the very heartstrings of the man I had said I do to. How could I know that he kept on loving her? It was in his actions, it was in all the times he could never tell me that he loved me, and it was in the words he kept stored away in a cedar chest. He would say, 'How could something that feels so right be so incredibly wrong?' He told of the times he held her and never wanted to let her go, that if she ever left him, his world would fall apart. Funny, neither of them knew that my world fell apart.

So what has come out of this, now that I am the last one standing? An unconditional love for my daughter and my husband's child, who, from the day she set foot in my house, became my child. The two of you were close and identical in so many ways because, as I liked to say, 'God got jokes.' You are my loves and no matter how you are related and what blood lines has brought you to be that way, you are the children of Deborah Price-Taylor and at the end of the day and when the trumpet sounds to call me home, that is all that will matter. I will never have to worry about you two taking care of each other, no matter where you go or what you do. God has promised me that you will always come back home.

By the time the last word was read, Cassie was crying uncontrollably, and so was I. It all made sense now, the special relationship I shared with Cassie and the loving way Mom protected us. And while it took all this time for it to come out, love is revealed many times in seasons. And this was our season of change.

After a while and when the tears stopped following we returned to the living room with the rest of our family. There were plans to make for the wedding, and a baby shower for Zee, who was seven months pregnant. We all were excited. It was as if all three of us were the mother of the one child she carried in her womb. What was even more special was, it was not conceived in the natural way, but with the help of science, and us together holding hands. She was confident and sure that Mr. Right would come, but in the meantime she would be a mother, which would give her enough joy to fill her heart.

Mom seemed at peace as I glanced out the corner of my eye and watched her and Cassie talk intently about one thing or another. Cassie would know happiness with Blaine. They were ready to start the rest of their life together. No one said anything about kids. I believed they were having too much fun just thinking about making them.

Then there was my husband. We had weathered the storm, and our relationship was stronger than it had ever been. We were still taking baby steps, so it was taking a while to get to where we wanted to be, but the trip was worth it all.

ORDER FORM
URBAN BOOKS, LLC
78 E. Industry Ct
Deer Park, NY 11729

Name: (please print):_____

Address: _____

City/State: _____

Zip: _____

QTY	TITLES	PRICE
	16 ½ On The Block	$14.95
	16 On The Block	$14.95
	Betrayal	$14.95
	Both Sides Of The Fence	$14.95
	Cheesecake And Teardrops	$14.95
	Denim Diaries	$14.95
	Happily Ever Now	$14.95
	Hell Has No Fury	$14.95
	If It Isn't love	$14.95
	Last Breath	$14.95
	Loving Dasia	$14.95
	Say It Ain't So	$14.95

Shipping and Handling - add $3.50 for 1st book then $1.75 for each additional book.

Please send a check payable to:

Urban Books, LLC

Please allow 4 - 6 weeks for delivery

ORDER FORM
URBAN BOOKS, LLC
78 E. Industry Ct
Deer Park, NY 11729

Name: (please print):_____

Address: _____

City/State: _____

Zip: _____

QTY	TITLES	PRICE
	The Cartel	$14.95
	The Cartel#2	$14.95
	The Dopeman's Wife	$14.95
	The Prada Plan	$14.95
	Gunz And Roses	$14.95
	Snow White	$14.95
	A Pimp's Life	$14.95
	Hush	$14.95
	Little Black Girl Lost 1	$14.95
	Little Black Girl Lost 2	$14.95
	Little Black Girl Lost 3	$14.95
	Little Black Girl Lost 4	$14.95

Shipping and Handling - add $3.50 for 1st book then $1.75 for each additional book.
Please send a check payable to:
Urban Books, LLC
Please allow 4 - 6 weeks for delivery

ORDER FORM
URBAN BOOKS, LLC
78 E. Industry Ct
Deer Park, NY 11729

Name: (please print):_____

Address: _____

City/State: _____

Zip: _____

QTY	TITLES	PRICE
	A Man's Worth	$14.95
	Abundant Rain	$14.95
	Battle Of Jericho	$14.95
	By The Grace Of God	$14.95
	Dance Into Destiny	$14.95
	Divorcing The Devil	$14.95
	Forsaken	$14.95
	Grace And Mercy	$14.95
	Guilty & Not Guilty Of Love	$14.95
	His Woman, His Wife His Widow	$14.95
	Illusion	$14.95
	The LoveChild	$14.95

Shipping and Handling - add $3.50 for 1st book then $1.75 for each additional book.
Please send a check payable to:
   Urban Books, LLC
Please allow 4 - 6 weeks for delivery

ORDER FORM
URBAN BOOKS, LLC
78 E. Industry Ct
Deer Park, NY 11729

Name: (please print):_____

Address: _____

City/State: _____

Zip: _____

QTY	TITLES	PRICE

Shipping and Handling - add $3.50 for 1st book then $1.75 for each additional book.

Please send a check payable to:

Urban Books, LLC

Please allow 4 - 6 weeks for delivery

Notes

Notes